Trust Me:
Brie's Submission

By
Red Phoenix

Trust Me: Brie's Submission #8
Copyright © 2016 by Red Phoenix
Print Edition

RedPhoenix69@live.com

Edited by Amy Parker, Proofed by Becki Wyer & Marilyn Cooper
Cover by CopperLynn
Phoenix symbol by Nicole Delfs

*Previously published as part of *Brie Masters Love in Submission*
Adult Reading Material (18+)

Dedication

Much love and thanks to my beautiful family
and my incredibly sexy husband.

I want to give a special shout-out to those fans who have
been with me since the beginning.
Your support of my work and my many characters blesses
this Phoenix more than I can express.
Your friendship and loyalty over the years has changed
the course of my life.
Hugs!

CONTENTS

Never

Numerous times during the lengthy international flight, Sir slid his hand behind her back and lightly pulled on the belt under her dress. It hit just the right spot to cause a pleasant pressure in her loins, which further teased and excited her.

"Tweaking the details," he murmured in her ear, "and later today I will grab on to that belt and fuck you like a slut, téa."

She shivered, smiling to herself. Yes, Sir was an expert at tweaking the details.

It was a surprise to Brie when they got through Russian security without any hassles. Even more surprising was the fact that Rytsar was nowhere to be found once they were out.

"He's still not answering his cell," Sir griped as he thrust his phone into his pocket. "I guess we'll take a cab."

Sir lifted his hand to hail one. It took a while before a taxi finally pulled up. While Brie climbed into the vehicle, the driver put their luggage into the trunk and asked Sir where they were headed. The instant Sir stated the address, the man's face fell. Without explanation, he unloaded the luggage and shook his head.

Sir spoke to the man in Russian, but he just kept repeating, "*Nyet*." He gestured Brie out of his cab, then sped off as if the hounds of hell were following him.

"Well, that was odd." Sir put his arm around Brie as he hailed another one.

After a few minutes, another cab pulled up. Before Sir let him take the luggage, he explained where he wanted to go. This cabbie looked alarmed, glancing around nervously before jumping into his vehicle and driving off with no explanation.

"Okay, now I am getting irritated," Sir complained. "What is Durov up to?"

Sir hailed a third cab and explained where they were headed. The cabbie hesitated for a moment, but then nodded. Sir breathed a sigh of relief. "Good. Keep your eyes open—Durov has to be around here someplace laughing his Ruski ass off."

The cabbie exited the airport, but was silent for the entire drive, even when Sir spoke to him directly. It was eerie.

"I don't understand where Durov is going with this ruse, but I don't find it particularly funny. Do you?"

Brie shook her head. "Not at all, Sir."

She felt chills as they rounded the corner of Rytsar's street and she heard Sir's intake of breath. She couldn't see anything yet and asked, "What is it?"

He did not respond, a frozen expression of shock on his face. As they pulled up to Rytsar's mansion, Brie understood why. The top half of the structure was gone, looking as if it had been physically ripped off, and what was left had been gutted by fire.

The cabbie quickly unloaded the luggage and demanded payment. Without counting the money or even looking back, he jumped back into the cab and hit the gas, leaving them standing in front of the ruins.

The shock of the scene held Brie speechless as she took in the devastation. She shook her head, not wanting to believe it. She followed silently behind Sir as he walked around the mansion. The back of it told the story. The entire side had been blown away as if by some tremendous explosion. Sir walked through the huge hole, carefully stepping over the rubble.

Brie finally found her voice and asked, "Do you think Rytsar survived?"

"I don't know."

"What's happened, Sir? What could have caused this?"

"It looks like a bomb but, as far as I know, Durov didn't have any enemies."

"Is it possible he got tangled up with the Russian mafia?"

"The Durov family does not engage in *Bratva* activities."

"Could he have become a target because of that?"

Sir's voice was empty when he answered. "I can't say." He walked farther inside, trying to make sense of the destruction around them.

"Rytsar..." Brie whimpered.

"This wasn't survivable," Sir stated dully.

"But he must have gotten out," Brie insisted, needing Sir to reassure her.

"I haven't heard from him for three days." Sir closed his eyes, his breathing becoming labored.

Brie grabbed on to him, tears falling silently as she glanced around at the burnt wreckage that had once been Rytsar's home. "He can't…"

"If this is related to the *Bratva*, then it explains the strange behavior of the cab drivers." Sir put his arm protectively around Brie. "We need to leave—we're not safe here."

"But we have to find out what happened to Rytsar," she cried desperately.

Sir grabbed her shoulders and shook her. "No one could survive this."

Brie's lip trembled.

He let go of her, the look of devastation on his face gutting her. Sir looked around the ruins, shaking his head in disbelief. "He's gone…"

"But not forgotten," a jovial voice announced behind them.

Brie turned around, her mouth agape as Rytsar walked up, a huge grin on his face. "It was truly beautiful to see your heartfelt concern for your old comrade, but not to fear. I am alive and well."

Sir stared at him for several seconds before he punched Rytsar square in the face. The large Russian crashed to the ground.

"You never joke about that!"

Rytsar's entourage advanced on Sir, ready to restrain him, but Rytsar got back to his feet, rubbing his jaw slowly. "Stop, no need," he said, calling back his guards.

Sir's eyes burned with anger as he stared down the Russian Dom.

"I'm so touched, *moy droog*. You—"

"You *never* joke about death." Sir turned away, his jaw quivering slightly.

Rytsar's jovial expression disappeared. "I'm sorry…" He tried to touch Sir's shoulder, but he jerked away from the Russian.

"Never."

Rytsar nodded. "You're right. It was a cruel joke." He reached out and grabbed Sir in a bear hug, refusing to let go. "I am heartily sorry."

Sir let out an angry sigh. "Don't ever fuck with me like that again."

Rytsar pulled back to look him in the eyes. "It was only meant in jest, but I won't, *moy droog*. I give my solemn promise."

Sir pushed him away, straightening his jacket with quick, jerky movements. "See that you don't."

Rytsar turned to Brie next, brushing away the remaining tears from her cheeks. "I apologize to you as well, *radost moya*. I did not appreciate how deeply you felt."

"Liar," Sir snarled.

The Russian Dom shook his head sadly. "I did not mean to cause a rift between us, brother."

Sir's lip twitched. "I don't forgive you, but I will look past this."

"Good, because I lost everything when the gas main exploded," Rytsar said, gesturing at the ruins around him.

Sir nodded in new understanding. "So that's what happened here."

"That's terrible, Rytsar," Brie cried. "What a horrible loss for you."

"Generations lost," he growled angrily.

Brie remembered all the heirlooms, the fine paintings, numerous antiques—the sheer amount of history that had been lost in the explosion was devastating.

"Mercifully, it happened on a Sunday when my staff were away," he explained.

"Where were you?" Brie asked.

He raised his eyebrow. "I was…occupied at the time."

She blushed and looked down at her feet, trying to hide her smile.

"Certain friends of mine pressured the local government to rebuild it, since a home of such rich historical significance was destroyed due to a faulty gas line. Construction will start once the area has been shored up and deemed safe. It is a testament to my forefathers that the foundation of my ancestral home remains solid."

"What about the items lost in the fire, Durov?" Sir asked.

Rytsar snorted in satisfaction. "I am being adequately compensated."

"But all your family heirlooms, all those memories…" Brie lamented.

"*Da,* but something of great value to me was spared."

"Really?" Sir remarked with interest.

Rytsar started walking farther into the interior of the building, waving his hand for them to follow.

Brie turned to Sir. "Is it safe?"

"Probably not."

Sir followed the Russian anyway, and since he hadn't forbidden Brie, she followed behind him.

"As you know, Father and I never had much in common, but even he would have been pleased."

Rytsar led them down what remained of the stairs and opened the thick door that led down to the dungeon. Brie gasped as she stepped inside. It looked completely untouched, as pristine as the day she'd visited it last. The walls were lined with lit torches, hinting at the fact that he'd planned to show them this little 'miracle' all along.

"I can't believe it's unscathed, considering the violence of the explosion," Sir said in amazement.

"It is truly a *chudo*," Rytsar agreed. He walked over to the wall of instruments. "My men have been thorough in checking for damage, but have yet to report any. I have, however, discovered one pleasant byproduct left by the fire that raged above." He picked up his cat o' nines and dragged it under his nose, breathing in deeply. "All of my instruments retain the scent of the smoke. I find it an alluring addition."

He held out the cat o' nines to Brie. "Wouldn't you agree?"

Brie walked over to take a whiff, but her body shivered being so close to the instrument, having experienced its ferocious bite. She smelled the leather, taking in the aroma, and looked up at him in surprise. "I do find it pleasing."

He caressed the cat o' nines sensually and asked, "Would you like another session, *radost moya*?"

Brie backed up to Sir, distancing herself from the Russian. "No, once was more than enough. Thank you."

Sir chuckled. "I think you have effectively cured my sub of that desire."

Rytsar put the tool back on the wall. "Such a shame," he said wistfully, stroking the length of it. "It's one of my favorite pastimes."

"So, Durov, where have you been staying since the explosion?"

"I have several apartments in Moscow. Housing is not a problem, only an inconvenience."

Brie crinkled her brow in confusion, wondering why he would have multiple residences when he lived in a mansion.

"There's still one thing I can't wrap my head around," Sir said. "Why did the drivers behave so strangely at the airport? It makes no sense, given that this was only a gas explosion."

Rytsar slapped him on the back, laughing. "I informed the taxi companies of your arrival and offered a healthy sum if they refused to take you. All but one driver, of course. Were they convincing? I promised an extra bonus if they were."

"Yes, Durov, they were," Sir stated dryly. "You should dig deep into your wallet. I hope it hurts."

"That is good to hear," he answered with a satisfied grin.

When Sir frowned, Rytsar immediately realized his

folly and said, "Let's forget the unpleasantness and concentrate on the rest of your stay here. I assume you will be headed to the cabin."

"Actually, I had planned to stay at your home. Because of what's happened, I suppose I can send Brie ahead until my business in Moscow is completed."

"Excellent! I will act as her host while you stay at my apartment, *moy droog.*"

Sir eyed him suspiciously. "Before I let you have her, I'll have to write down a list of what you can and cannot do in my absence."

"Only if you feel a list is necessary."

"Imperative."

"Don't you trust your longtime comrade?"

"After this last stunt? No."

"That hurts," Rytsar said, placing his hand over his heart. "But I will make it up to you both," he promised solemnly. "Come—we will stuff our bellies, drink a bottle or two of vodka, and go over this list together."

Pink or Blue

Rytsar took them to the modern side of Moscow, famous for its towering skyscrapers and twisted glass buildings that looked more like art than offices.

"Moscow is such a cool city," Brie exclaimed, looking up at the tall structures, in awe of their varied architectural design.

"It is a rare gem among the great cities," Rytsar stated proudly. "Moscow has a long and rich history."

He took them to a newly built apartment building made of glass and steel. It was a marvel of modern conveniences and artful design—the exact opposite of the historic mansion he'd grown up in.

"I can better understand why you have multiple dwellings, Rytsar," Brie said, adding, "it gives you the chance to enjoy the old and the new."

"*Da*, I truly had the best of both worlds," he agreed sadly.

Brie realized that she'd just stuck her foot in her mouth by mentioning the mansion, but before she could apologize, he changed the subject. "To go along with that theme, there is a new restaurant that opened recently. Let me tantalize you with the traditional foods of my forefathers, tweaked with a modern flair."

She eagerly agreed, as she took a moment to survey his spacious apartment. The windows overlooking the scenic downtown reminded Brie of Sir's home, but instead of art covering the walls, Rytsar's place was decorated with BDSM tools, many of which looked cruel and menacing. As she glanced at the various instruments, she couldn't help wondering if they were strictly for ornamentation or actual use.

Rytsar kept his word and they did end up stuffing themselves, but Brie never got to partake of the vodka. A full stomach, after a long plane trip and an emotional scare, had her drifting off before the night had even started.

Brie was bereft when she woke up in an empty bed early the next morning.

"Sir?"

When she got no answer, Brie slipped out from under the covers, and was flustered to discover she was completely naked. She looked around the room, grateful when she spied her clothes folded on a chair. She trusted that Sir had been the one to undress her but wondered, *Why didn't he join me in bed?*

After donning her clothes, she peeked her head out of the room. There sat Sir and Rytsar, chatting away with glasses of vodka in their hands.

"Drinking in the morning, Sir?" she chided playfully when she emerged from the bedroom.

He looked at his watch and winked at her. "Nope, we never stopped."

Rytsar nudged Sir and asked, "Want to toast to the morning?"

"Why not?"

Rytsar poured two large glasses.

Brie stared at them in shock, surprised that they had nearly finished off two bottles of vodka. "What did you two do all night, besides drink?"

"There was much discussion, my little sub." Sir took the glass Rytsar handed him, and picked up a pickle before toasting. "To my bastard of a friend, who doesn't deserve to lick my boots."

Rytsar's low laughter filled the apartment. "To my grouchy comrade, who needs to find where he misplaced his humor."

The two clinked glasses and chugged. It was perversely interesting to watch, considering how much vodka was already flowing in their veins. They slammed the glasses down and consumed their pickles with gusto.

Sir turned to Brie afterwards. "I'm glad to see you're awake. I've missed your presence."

Brie knelt on the floor beside him and laid her head on his lap, purring when he began stroking her hair. "I'm sorry I missed your conversations, Sir."

"It was for the best, *radost moya*," Rytsar assured her.

Brie didn't feel that way at all. She wanted to learn everything there was to know about these two, and knew vodka made them unusually open and talkative. "So…what *did* you discuss, Master?" she asked provocatively, rubbing her hand against his inner thigh.

He looked down at her with a mischievous smile that hinted at secrets unknown. "We talked about our college days and a certain list that needed to be made…"

"Oh, you tease me so."

"I like to keep you on your toes, téa. It keeps you strong and focused."

She turned to Rytsar. "He definitely keeps me on my toes. Did he tell you about his latest challenge at the commune?"

Rytsar nodded. "I could imagine your pussy quivering for a stranger as he lubed up his cock for you."

"It wasn't just my pussy that was quivering." Brie laid her head back on Sir's thigh. "But my Master never steers me in the wrong direction. I trust him completely."

"It is equally met, little sub," Sir replied, lifting her chin. "You force me to face emotions I'm unwilling to confront."

"We're the perfect team," she said, kissing his hand.

"I would find you two sickening but for the fact you are my good friends."

Sir chuckled. "I would find us nauseating as well. However…" He paused, looking down at Brie. "I can't get enough of her."

Rytsar held up the nearly empty bottle of vodka, but Sir declined. The Russian poured the last of it into his glass and downed it. He snapped his fingers, and from seemingly out of nowhere, his bodyguard, Titov, produced two packages.

"As you know, I have been waiting for this day with impatience ever since you told me you had news to share, *moy droog.*" He added with a glint in his eye, "It's taken you long enough."

Rytsar nodded to the guard, and the man handed Brie one of the gifts. She tore at it excitedly, wondering what pre-wedding surprise he had picked out for them. She was a tad shocked when she pulled out a tiny dress of excessive pink lace.

Brie couldn't help but laugh, and shook her head at him.

"No?" he asked in surprise. "Not a problem." The bodyguard handed her the second gift and Brie dutifully opened it.

It was a miniature tux of blue. Brie blushed, shaking her head again.

Rytsar looked utterly devastated and turned to Sir. "No *malyshka?*"

Sir stood up and put his hand on the Russian's shoulder. "No, my friend. I was simply going to ask you to be the best man at my wedding."

Rytsar gave Sir a look of disgust, then turned to Brie with a charming grin. "*Radost moya*, you would have a round belly and we would be anticipating our first *dotchka* if you were mine."

Brie giggled. "Rytsar, I'm not ready to have babies yet!" She held up both baby outfits and shrugged. "Seriously, I'm only twenty-three and I have a film career to think about."

Rytsar motioned her to him. Brie stood up and

walked over, leaning close when he said in a secretive tone, "The sooner you start your little family, the sooner they fly the nest." He added for emphasis, "Your Master isn't getting any younger."

"I heard that."

"I only speak the truth, *moy droog*. If your little sub is to stand any chance of being a mother, you need to start making your fucking count."

Brie burst out in a giggle.

"I think I will withdraw your best man status," Sir snarled.

"If you are a man who cannot handle the truth, then yes, by all means withdraw the honor," Rytsar challenged with a wicked grin.

"If you are so anxious for children, why not impregnate one of your subs? I'm sure there are several who would be happy to carry your child."

Rytsar shook his head. "I'm far too young for such commitment, but not to be a *dyadya*."

"You're a year older than me, my friend."

"Ah, but you have found 'the one' and I have not. A child should be conceived in love, no?"

Sir grunted in agreement.

Rytsar held his massive arms out as if he were cradling a baby. "To hold and spoil a tiny version of *radost moya*..." he said wistfully.

"And if it's a boy?" Sir questioned.

"It won't be."

"All this talk of babies has me craving a pickle," Brie said, grabbing one off the tray and munching on it.

"The day you refuse my vodka is the day I'll know

you are pregnant." Rytsar snapped his fingers and Titov fetched a new bottle. "Will you have a drink with me?"

Brie looked at Sir.

"Do as you wish."

Not wanting to be left out, Brie nodded. "Please, Rytsar."

"Although that is not the answer I wanted, I am pleased to fill your glass. Zyr has become my vodka of choice. Let me know what you think."

She downed the fiery alcohol at the same time as Rytsar, surprised that it went down so smoothly, far more easily than she'd been expecting, with only a hint of bitterness afterwards.

"What do you think, *radost moya*?"

She smiled. "It's surprisingly smooth!"

He held his pickle to his lips, so she did the same and they both bit down on the salty treats. Brie giggled as she chewed on the pickle while looking into Rytsar's eyes.

"Do you think you can handle Durov for a couple of days?" Sir asked her.

Brie turned to her Master and replied solemnly, "If he has agreed to the terms you have set, then yes. I trust your judgment completely." She embraced the warmth the vodka caused and added proudly, "I would do anything you asked, Sir."

"Count yourself lucky I do not have a wicked heart, because that statement could get you in a lot of trouble, Miss Bennett," Sir teased.

Brie liked the easy banter that alcohol seemed to bring about.

"I will make the best of the limited access I've been

afforded," Rytsar murmured resentfully.

"A tight rein is the only way I would allow you control over her. I know you, Durov."

"*Da*. At least you have agreed to the club."

Brie's interest was piqued. "Club?"

Rytsar's grin was roguishly intimidating. "A favorite underground BDSM club of mine, with a decidedly sadistic slant."

Brie turned to Sir in surprise, her mouth agape.

"You did just say you would do anything I asked."

She trembled as she nodded.

"My requirements of Durov are very specific."

"Too restrictive," Rytsar complained.

Sir assured Brie, "You will not be compromised, but you will be tested." He handed Rytsar all the items off the coffee table one by one, then commanded her in a sensuous tone, "Undress and lie on the table for me, téa."

Brie smiled as she slowly removed her clothes for her Master, wanting to entice them both with her disrobing without making it a blatant striptease, which Sir had not asked for.

He helped her onto the table and ran his hand over her body. "I think we bite her."

Rytsar moved to the other side. "Agreed."

Brie held her breath as both men leaned down and took a bite of her thighs. Neither was gentle as they bruised her skin between their teeth, and she gasped.

"Too much?" Sir asked.

"No, Master."

"I will start at her toes, you go for the neck," Sir instructed his friend.

Brie whimpered when Rytsar stared at her with those penetrating blue eyes before nestling his warm lips against her throat. He started out so tender, lightly kissing and teasing…

The instant Sir bit down on her sensitive arch, Rytsar sank his teeth into her, sucking hard as he bit. The dual sensations at opposite ends were too much, and she instinctively tried to twist out of their reach.

Strong hands held her down, her action only inciting more of their delightfully cruel play. Brie whimpered as Rytsar took samples of her neck, breasts and torso as Sir moved from her toes to her thighs and up to her quivering pussy.

They licked, nipped and bruised her most sensitive areas with those wicked teeth, making her crazy with desire even as she squirmed beneath them to avoid the momentary pinpoints of pain.

Master knew her attraction to being bitten, but to be bitten by these two men—to be marked by their passion—what more could a girl want?

With a husky voice, Sir announced, "She's exceedingly wet."

"We may have a masochist yet," Rytsar said, biting harder until she yelped. Brie shook her head. He chuckled as he moved to a new spot to torture with his lips and teeth.

Sir rimmed her wet opening and she moaned in pleasure as he slipped two fingers inside, but Brie soon stiffened when Rytsar's fingers pushed their way in too, stretching her tight.

It so closely reminded her of Mary's encounter that her pussy began to pulsate in response to their attention.

"No coming, téa."

Brie groaned as she fought off the urge while both men forced their fingers deeper inside her. She was ravenous to be overfilled by them, and bucked her hips upwards. They obliged her need and began pumping her in unison, rubbing vigorously against her G-spot.

She instantly realized her mistake and tried to pull away, but Rytsar dug his fingers into her waist, preventing her escape.

Brie tossed her head back and forth, and begged them to stop. "Please, no more. No more, Master…"

Neither man listened to her desperate pleas. In a last-ditch effort, Brie stilled herself and tried to concentrate on a spot on the ceiling. She *almost* succeeded, until each man grasped one of her wrists with his free hand and bit down on her sensitive skin.

She. Was. Lost.

Brie came hard, her body clamping down on the four fingers inside her as her pussy gushed with watery come.

Tears rolled down her cheeks from the intensity of her climax and the knowledge that she had failed to obey Sir's command. She lowered her hips to the table in resignation as they pulled out their wet fingers and looked at each other, saying nothing.

What will happen to me now?

"Why did you disobey me?"

Brie did not offer any excuses. "I was greedy, Master."

Rytsar broke out in laughter. "I appreciate her honesty."

Sir couldn't hide his smile as she explained, "I wanted it too much and then I couldn't stop myself when I needed to pull back."

"How shall we punish such wanton behavior, téa?"

Brie swallowed, unsure if her answer would be well received but feeling too giddy to stop herself. "Make me come again?"

This time Sir was the one who laughed.

"You have a cheeky sub, *moy droog*," Rytsar said, chuckling along with him, but then he became scary-serious. "She must be punished."

The smile on Brie's lips disappeared when Sir replied, "I agree, Durov."

Brie whimpered as each man undid his buckle and slid his belt from his pants. "I'm sorry, Master. I was trying to be funny. Please…"

"What you consider humor, I call insolence," Rytsar replied coldly. "This will hurt you far more than it will hurt me. Kneel on the table with your hands behind your neck."

Brie looked at Sir and he nodded. Shocked by the turn of events, she pulled herself up into a kneeling position and clasped her hands behind her—her whole body shaking with fear.

Instead of hitting her with the belt, Sir fastened his around her neck, pulling tightly so that she felt the constrictive pressure of it.

"That is a pretty picture," Rytsar complimented.

Sir reached over and pulled on the belt, forcing her head back. He kissed her deeply, keeping his hold on the belt so that she felt the pressure and knew who was in control.

Damn if her pussy didn't pulsate with desire. She was hopeless in the hands of these two.

Rytsar forcibly bound her knees together with his belt, announcing, "There will be no more release for you."

The men unzipped their pants and presented her with their rigid cocks.

"You will pleasure us at the same time."

Brie beamed inside, realizing they'd only been teasing her, but she continued to act the part of a repentant submissive. She gazed up at them with a remorseful expression, eager to pay for her disobedience.

Grasping both shafts, she began stroking and was rewarded by their low grunts of pleasure. Her pussy ached with sexual desire. She leaned over and licked the pre-come from Sir's cock, then began sucking his shaft while keeping the same rhythm with her hand as she stroked Rytsar.

The luxury of two cocks was deliciously extravagant, and Brie moaned as she moved to Rytsar's shaft, not wanting either man to feel neglected. She looked up as she took him into her mouth.

Rytsar did not move or make a sound as he watched her. It was unnerving, the way he gazed at her so intensely. She knew she'd failed to please him orally the first time they'd scened together, and was determined to show him the full extent of her expertise.

Brie relaxed her throat and took his shaft deeper. Still there was no reaction from the man, just an intensive stare that challenged her. What more did he want?

Her attention to Rytsar did not go unnoticed by her Master, who pulled on the belt around her neck. She disengaged from the Russian and returned to Sir. He pulled back her head as he applied pressure to the belt.

"The challenge is to please us both at the same time," he reminded her. "Not an easy task."

She nodded, amping up her hand motion on Rytsar's cock as she flicked her tongue under the ridge of Sir's shaft.

"Deeper," he commanded.

Brie opened her lips wide and took his entirety.

"Good girl..." he growled.

Brie moaned on his shaft, loving his praise. She added a little twist to her wrist action with Rytsar so he would know she hadn't forgotten him, and was rewarded with a release of pre-come. It lubed his cock, allowing for more energetic handling.

Sir pulled on her belt, forcing her to disengage.

Brie stroked his manhood, using the twisting motion as she returned to the Russian. She started down at his balls, licking, nipping and sucking her way up the length of his shaft. Although his expression remained stoic, she noticed a slight upturn at the corner of his mouth. It was all she needed...

Brie took him into her mouth and began slowly taking him deeper, making him anticipate the constriction of her tight throat around his shaft. She played him as she continued to stroke Sir's shaft vigorously. Opposite ends of the spectrum—one slow and deliberate, the other fast and furious.

When her lips encircled the base of his shaft, Rytsar actually let out a low groan as he looked down at her.

Triumph!

She slowly pulled away from him and returned to Sir. It pleased her greatly to tease Rytsar as she took her Master deep, giving him what Rytsar had only tasted for a moment.

Brie took the fullness of Sir's shaft to the base and then did her signature shallow pumping to tighten her throat around him.

"That's it, babygirl."

She changed the rhythm of her stroking of Rytsar to match the movements of her mouth on Sir's cock. Slow, deep, gentle…

"*Hvatit,*" Rytsar snarled under his breath.

Without warning, he pulled on the belt, prying her from Sir's cock. He then forcefully guided her lips onto his shaft and held her head with both hands as he pumped her mouth.

So much for teasing the sadist.

Brie relaxed her throat and looked up at him, taking his hard thrusts with the same grace she'd seen Mary achieve.

I am your vessel of pleasure…

But she had not forgotten her Master, and stroked his shaft with the same intensity that Rytsar was pumping her mouth. She knew that as Sir watched, the sensations of her hand would mimic the feeling of being deep-throated.

"Fuucckkk…" Sir groaned.

Rytsar pulled away from her and commanded,

"Stroke it until I come."

She stroked both men with long, tightfisted caresses. She opened her mouth and stuck her tongue out in anticipation and was rewarded with their tangy release. She licked the heads of their cocks, taking as much of their seed as she could. Her chin and breasts were covered in their white reward by the end, despite her best efforts, and the fresh smell of come filled her nostrils. Brie moaned in satisfaction, grateful for the honor.

Sir pulled on the belt and she tilted her head up to look at him.

"Go clean up, babygirl, and present yourself to me when you're done."

Rytsar undid the belt around her knees while Sir released her from the one on her throat. She felt a sense of loss when it slid from her, appreciating the submissive feeling the belt had evoked.

Before Rytsar let her leave, he pulled her to him and murmured, "You are much improved, *radost moya*. Much improved…" She blushed as a smile crept across her lips—gratified that he had noticed her enhanced skills.

Brie hurried down the hallway to the bathroom to take a quick shower, readying herself for more play. She was curious what else the two had in mind, but was disappointed when she returned to discover Rytsar lying on the couch, snoring.

Sir was nowhere to be seen, so she headed to the bedroom and found him lying on the bed working on his laptop.

He saw the disappointment on her face and smiled,

motioning her over to him. "Losing his ancestral home has affected Durov more than he will admit. It's exacting an emotional toll he refuses to acknowledge."

"He's lost so much," Brie agreed, curling up beside Sir on the bed.

"Having you here will prove a good distraction. I've asked him to take you out tonight to film a session with one of his subs."

"Thank you, Sir. Will you be joining us too?"

He chuckled. "No, I'll be sleeping." He stroked her hair and Brie felt the familiar tingles down her back start.

She glanced at his computer screen, but it meant nothing to her because it was written in Russian. The fact that he was fluent in the language was just another aspect about Sir she admired.

As the minutes passed, her curiosity got the best of her and she asked, "When did you learn Russian, Sir? Before or after you met Rytsar?"

He said nonchalantly, as if it were a common occurrence, "Soon after I met Durov. It only seemed natural once we became blood brothers."

Brie shook her head, now with a million more questions she wanted to ask, but Sir put his finger on her lips. "I'm not up for a question and answer session right now, Brie. I suggest you plan out tonight's shoot. Rytsar said he was open to anything you wanted to see."

It was with great effort that Brie switched gears, her head still swimming with the knowledge that Rytsar and Sir had a rich history she knew little about. She hoped the Russian would be more forthcoming about their past once she got him alone.

Brie grabbed a pad and pencil from the nightstand and snuggled up to Sir, grateful to have this quiet time together. The fact he enjoyed her presence as much as she enjoyed his was of great comfort to her.

Wicked Sadist

Rytsar was raring to show off his skills for the camera, and wasted no time once he had awakened from his nap. Brie shared her ideas for the scene, but he disagreed.

"No, we start with something simple. It is always best to start that way."

She shrugged. "You're the expert, but I *had* hoped for footage that people wouldn't be able to stop talking about."

He smiled confidently. "No need to fret, *radost moya*."

His guard, Titov, escorted Brie into the vehicle and then loaded all of her equipment, while Rytsar called to make the necessary arrangements with two of his subs. Brie was taken to an apartment on the other side of Moscow.

"One of my girls is setting up the scene at my old apartment so we can begin immediately," he informed her.

"Great," Brie answered, forcing herself to calm the nerves that had started. She wondered how she would handle watching Rytsar from behind the camera lens. This was a first for both of them.

His sub met them at the door and bowed low at Rytsar's feet. Without verbally greeting her, he touched the sub on the head on his way in as acknowledgement, then began barking commands. The older woman rocked off her heels and quietly closed the door before responding to his numerous requests.

Brie looked around the apartment, noting how small but comfortable it was, with female touches such as flowers on the kitchen table, frilly pillows on the couch and paintings of animals on the walls. Not Rytsar's tastes at all. She wondered if this was a 'perk' to being one of Rytsar's preferred subs.

While the sub busied herself with last-minute details, Brie got out her equipment and starting positioning the reflectors. Rytsar disappeared into the bedroom, leaving the women to their respective jobs. They worked together in silence, but Brie was struck by how comfortable she felt in the presence of the woman, despite their language, age and fetish differences. His submissive seemed almost regal in the way she held herself, but there was no arrogance radiating from her. Rytsar certainly had good taste in women.

The Russian Dom came out a short time later, dressed only in brown leather pants and dark boots. Brie had to admit the dragon tattoo stood out prominently on his left shoulder, only adding to his sex appeal. She was convinced the audience would love him.

When the doorbell rang, Rytsar turned to Brie. "Start filming. Say nothing, just observe what I do. I will explain as I go."

Brie nodded, her heart racing as he opened the door to a young, petite woman. The first thing Brie noticed was her stunning crystal-blue eyes and sensually arched eyebrows. The girl looked to be the same age as Brie, a sharp contrast to the other sub in the room.

Rytsar invited her inside, speaking in Russian. The two seemed to have a casual vanilla conversation as she undressed down to her underwear in front of him. He wasn't even looking at her as they spoke, because he was too busy preparing his instruments for the scene.

The way they interacted was so relaxed that Brie imagined they were talking about the weather or some equally mundane topic. She got so caught up in listening to the lilt of their conversation that she was caught off-guard when the girl suddenly bowed and he directed his other sub to grab her wrists.

What had started out as vanilla and routine quickly took on a kinky tone, as the new girl was forced onto her feet and dragged to the St. Andrew's cross in the corner of the room. Rytsar explained to Brie, "She does not care for other women, and wishes I would bind her to the cross myself." His smile was dangerously charming when he added, "However...I prefer to see her challenged. She needs to be reminded who's in control."

Rytsar walked up to the girl and spoke to her in English, although it was obvious from her blank reaction that the sub couldn't understand a word he'd said. It reminded Brie of her first encounter with Rytsar when he'd only spoken to her in Russian—adding an element of mystery and intrigue to their initial scene together.

Brie could appreciate how it was adding to this sub's experience. Being filmed by an American she didn't know while her Master spoke to her in that foreign language—it was the stuff fantasies were made of.

Rytsar smiled at the girl as he murmured tenderly, "Ksana, you and I have a unique relationship. Your extremely low tolerance for pain makes our scenes together far too short, and yet…unbearably sweet."

The other submissive barked a command and the girl obediently lifted her arm to be secured to the cross.

Rytsar told Brie, "It turns me on to watch her willingly give herself over to my submissive, despite her inner objection, simply because ksana knows it pleases me."

He walked around the cross, taking in the erotic scene of the nearly naked submissive being bound to the wooden cross by another of his women. Brie could appreciate the sensual power play this was for the Dom. He certainly knew how to push boundaries while still making his submissive hungry to please him. Brie had experienced it herself, and was inspired by the sexual confidence he was showing now.

Rytsar explained, "Whereas ksana has a low tolerance for pain, Dessa has a very high tolerance. It allows me to release my passion without fear of harming her. In fact, Dessa and I can play for hours. Can't we, my sweet?" he stated proudly, caressing the older woman's cheek. "Lift your dress so they can admire our last play session."

Unlike the girl, this sub understood English, and stopped the binding process to lift her dress above her head. She turned her back to the camera to show off her marks.

Brie had to hold in her gasp as she focused the camera's lens on the dark red marks covering the woman's shoulders and curvaceous buttocks. Just seeing them caused goosebumps on Brie's skin.

"Aren't they beautiful?" Rytsar stated affectionately, lightly caressing the marks he'd left during a previous session.

Dessa smiled at Rytsar after pulling down her dress, and he kissed her tenderly before leaving her to return to her task of binding the girl.

Rytsar approached ksana with a ball gag in his hand. "You will be screaming, slave, and we don't want to disturb our neighbors." He lifted the large rubber ball to her mouth. "Open."

The girl didn't have to understand English to know what he wanted. She opened her beautiful pink lips and accepted the gag, her chest rising and falling rapidly as he secured it around her head.

Rytsar turned to Brie. "She's scared. She knows I will hurt her today, and yet she cannot resist the craving. It is…intoxicating for us both."

He stood back to admire her. The girl's nipples were hard, indicating both her fear and anticipation. "You look exquisite bound to my cross, as you wait for my pleasure."

Rytsar left her to pick up an instrument Brie had never seen before. The long, thin wand was red and triangular-like in shape, but she had no idea what it was used for. As soon as the submissive saw it, however, she started whimpering, struggling against her bonds as tears formed in her eyes.

Brie noticed that the girl's eyes were riveted to the tool when he turned it on. Rytsar caressed the girl's wet cheek with his other hand. "Yes, you remember this wand well, don't you?"

He shared with Brie, "I allowed her to experience the jolt of the device last time we met, and she didn't care for it." He smiled, turning back to the girl and crooning softly, "Did you, pet?"

The girl shook like a leaf when he brought the tool near her face. She turned her head away, but her eyes remained locked on the tool.

Brie almost felt sorry for her, but reminded herself that ksana had come here to play, knowing full well Rytsar's brand of kink. She figured there must be some addictive aspect to the pain that this girl responded to. Why else would she choose not to end the scene when she was obviously terrified?

The Russian stroked ksana's cheek again and murmured, "She doesn't know it yet, but she will press her breast into it of her own free will today."

The girl whimpered in relief when he turned it off and put the instrument down, replacing it with the Magic Wand.

Brie felt her loins tingle pleasantly seeing the stimulating vibrator in his hand. The girl visibly relaxed as Rytsar knelt on one knee and placed the wand against her lacy panties, pressing it against her pussy. He looked up at his sub and said something in Russian.

The girl nodded.

Rytsar informed Brie, "I explained to ksana that

when she orgasms, it will signify her permission for me to continue with the other tool."

Brie licked her lips, now deliciously nervous for the girl. When Rytsar turned on the Magic Wand, its loud buzzing called to Brie. She sighed to herself, wishing she could partake in its wicked vibration.

Ksana closed her eyes, determined to resist the intense tool, but there was no escaping the vibrations, bound as she was. Rytsar growled seductively, saying aloud, "You cannot stop what is about to happen, pet. Fight all you want, but you *will* come for me, and when you do, I will ask you to press your sensitive nipple against the electric prod."

The girl whimpered when Rytsar turned the Magic Wand to the higher setting. She threw her head back, moaning as she fought against the building orgasm.

Rytsar grunted in satisfaction when her thighs began to quiver, and he said proudly, "See how she fights it? She knows that intense pain will follow her pleasure and it terrifies her, yet she is unwilling to prevent it."

All three watched silently as the girl shook her head, trying to stave off her impending orgasm. Her body became drenched in sweat from the effort as her thighs shook with more violence.

Rytsar boasted, "She's stubborn and I admire her for that. Fear of pain is a powerful motivator, but it also causes the orgasms to be that much more intense."

Brie was impressed by the girl's tenacity. There was no way she could have lasted as long under the relentless vibration of the Wand on its highest speed. Finally, there was a deep groan from the young sub as her body tensed for an orgasm that could not be denied.

Rytsar stared at the girl's mound with uninhibited lust.

Her cries were muffled by the large ball gag as she stiffened, just before a gush of juices soaked her panties and Rytsar's hand with her powerful climax. It was damn sexy to watch.

Afterwards, he stood up and picked up his wicked tool, turning it on. The girl started whimpering again.

"You know what you must do."

She stared at the tool, tears falling freely.

He put the instrument near ksana's left breast, her nipple poking through the thin material of her bra. Rytsar nodded his head towards it and smiled encouragingly to her.

The girl hesitated before lifting her shoulder so that her tender nipple came into contact with the end of the tool. Her muffled scream stirred something in Brie.

"Again," he told her, moving the device to her other breast.

The girl pleaded with her eyes, shaking her head, but Rytsar was silent as he waited patiently for her to comply.

The sub gulped between sobs as she slowly brought her right nipple into contact with the electricity.

"Good girl," Rytsar praised when her muted scream filled the apartment. He immediately turned off the device and grabbed her throat, biting her neck passionately. The girl seemed to melt into him, her tears suddenly forgotten.

"Turn off the camera, *radost moya*."

Brie pressed the off button as Rytsar took off the ball gag, wiping the excess spittle from ksana's mouth before bending down and releasing her ankles. He unbuttoned his pants and pulled out his hard shaft.

With her wrists still bound to the cross, he lifted her knees to her chest, then pushed aside the lacy material of her thong.

Holding her in that position, Rytsar penetrated her dripping-wet pussy. They both cried out in pleasure as he sank his cock deep into her and began thrusting. He growled something into her ear as he pounded the girl with a vengeance, his muscles churning from effort as he fucked her.

Good lord, that's how he looks when he takes me, Brie thought to herself.

She found it too erotic to watch, so Brie shifted her gaze towards the kitchen and thought of omelets…

The Lake

Rytsar drove with Brie to the cabin the next morning. It was difficult to leave Sir behind, the only consolation being that he would join them as soon as his meetings were finished.

"Be good, babygirl."

"I don't think I'm the one you have to worry about, Sir."

He chuckled and pulled her to him. "I'd trust that man with my life."

She stood on tiptoes and kissed her Master gently on the lips. "If you trust him, then I trust him."

"That isn't to say I didn't set strict parameters for Durov. I may trust him, but I'm not an idiot."

"I disagree," Rytsar stated, coming up behind them and slapping Sir hard on the back. "Based on your extensive list, there is little trust between you and I."

Sir laughed. "I relish the idea of you struggling to meet your needs under the confines of my limits."

"You are no friend."

Sir looked down at Brie. "I want you to be open to

his lessons, téa. He is not your Master in my absence, but I have given him permission to train you."

Brie's stomach did a flip. "I will do my best to learn, Master."

Sir played with the collar around her neck. "Be true to yourself—it's all I ask."

Tears filled her eyes. "I love you."

He kissed her, drawing out the tenderness of the connection before letting her go. "Until we meet again…"

Rytsar was unusually quiet on the drive up to the cabin. She wasn't sure if he was contemplating the days ahead or if he was preoccupied by the loss of his familial home. Either way, she wanted him to know she was there as support. She did not stare out of the window but sat quietly, her eyes on her lap but her focus completely on Rytsar.

He cleared his throat and took her hand, placing it on his muscular thigh. There was no other contact made and no words shared, but that simple act touched her deeply.

When they pulled up to the secluded cabin—his birthday gift to her—Brie let out a surprised gasp.

Rytsar smiled as one of his guards opened the door, and helped her out of the vehicle.

"What's this?" she asked the Russian Dom, staring at an elaborate wooden swing set with a big slide and jungle gym attached.

"I made the assumption my comrade had done right by you, and simply wanted my little niece to have her own swing set when she comes to visit her *dyadya*."

Brie burst out laughing. "Even if I were pregnant, it would be a while before she was old enough to use this."

He led her to the equipment. "Ah, but it is made strong enough for adults." He pointed her to one of the swings.

When Brie sat down on it, he began pushing her. She let out a trill of laughter, feeling as lighthearted as a child.

"I see that you enjoy my equipment, *radost moya*."

She grinned, noting the sexual innuendo behind the comment and answered, "Yes, I enjoy it very much, but that shouldn't surprise you."

Rytsar's eyes glinted with mischievous delight as he held the swing still and ordered her to follow him. They walked beside the shore of the lake in silence.

"Did your Master tell you what is on the list?" he asked.

Brie sighed nervously. "No, he didn't."

Rytsar nodded his head thoughtfully. He led her out onto a wooden pier, his expression solemn and somewhat frightening when he told her, "I was instructed to challenge you."

"I was afraid of that."

"One area in particular."

Brie swallowed hard, dreading his answer. "Which one?"

"Watersports."

She stared at him in shock. "But Sir knows I struggle

in that area."

"Precisely."

"It's not even something I'm interested in."

"I am quite aware of that."

Brie stared at the calm lake water, feeling anything but serene.

"You should know that your Master has kept that side of himself hidden, knowing how you feel."

She shifted uncomfortably beside him. It suddenly made sense that Sir hadn't explained what would happen at the cabin. He was ashamed of his own desires. Yet, it was a fetish she'd never imagined Sir enjoyed—not in a million years.

"It must be important to him," she mused out loud.

Rytsar said nothing.

Brie was put off by the idea of watersports and had no desire to pursue it. Still…if it was something that turned Sir on, shouldn't she at least keep an open mind? Wasn't that her duty as his collared submissive *and* lover?

"Be gentle with me, Rytsar," she pleaded. "You know this is uncomfortable territory for me."

"Gentle? I'm sorry, *radost moya*, I cannot be gentle."

Brie screamed when he swept her off her feet and tossed her into the water. She came up sputtering and gasping for air to the sound of Rytsar's boisterous laughter.

It wasn't until then that she understood. Brie ignored the hand he held out to her and swam all the way back to shore. She'd stomped halfway to the cabin before he caught up with her.

"Now, now…" he chuckled, encircling her in his

arms.

Brie struggled, but could not break free. She pounded his chest with her fists out of frustration. "That wasn't nice!"

The low timbre of Rytsar's laughter was sexy, but insulting in its mirth.

"I can't believe you did that to me," she cried, pounding harder.

Rytsar grabbed her wrists and held them up so that her face was inches from his. "I am not to blame, since I've been forced to derive pleasure based on the strict limits your Master's given me."

"But to joke about that?"

"Admit it was funny."

Brie shook her head violently, droplets spraying everywhere. "No, it wasn't!"

"It was," he insisted.

She looked up at him and repeated, "No, it wasn't."

"Watersports…"

Brie's frown slowly cracked into a smile against her will, as a drop of water traveled from her bangs down her cheek. "Yeah, watersports." She giggled as he escorted her to the cabin.

Before they reached the door, she asked, "Just so we're clear. You're not going to start peeing on me, right?"

He stopped and answered seriously, "Only if it would turn you on."

Rytsar said it with such conviction that she wondered if it was a kink he practiced himself. For a fraction of a second she actually considered it, but shook her head, shocked at his power over her.

She suspected that the Russian Dom could convince her to try anything, no matter her level of opposition. It made the man dangerous in her eyes.

Rytsar informed Brie that he was taking her to the underground BDSM club that evening. "Part of the reason I chose to buy this particular plot of land was the proximity to the club which meets a half-hour from here." He chuckled wickedly. "This is like nothing you are used to in America. It's been in existence for over a hundred years and distinguishes itself with its authoritarian rules."

Brie was intimidated at the thought of facing such a foreign environment, terrified that she would fail. She was desperate not to disappoint Rytsar—or Sir. "What are the protocols?" she asked him. "Just how authoritarian are they?"

Rytsar chuckled again, enjoying her discomfort far too much. "In this club you must stand three feet behind me, and keep your gaze down at all times. They will respect your collar, but won't hesitate to physically punish any sub who steps out of line."

Brie's anxiety increased two-fold.

"No need to worry," he said soothingly. "Unless, of course, you forget yourself and make eye contact."

"You're not helping," Brie groaned. "You know what a challenge that is for me." She looked at him suspiciously and asked, "This isn't another one of your jokes?"

Rytsar shook his head. "No, *radost moya*, this is very serious. I will not be able to protect you if you insult one of the other Dominants at the club."

"Why take me, then?"

"Were you not the top of your class at the Submissive Training Center?"

His question both challenged and grounded her. Brie hadn't been in a formal setting in months, but she understood her place. Although she was afraid of accidentally breaking protocol, she was a competent submissive. She smiled at him, feeling her confidence grow when she answered, "Yes, I was."

"They will be observing your every move tonight."

The thought of accidentally making a mistake and being punished by a sadist frightened her. Rytsar read the fear playing across her face and grasped her chin, forcing her to look into his pale blue eyes.

"It is very simple. Keep your gaze focused on the heel of my boots, and your hands behind your back. Do not speak. Although my friends will be admiring your body, they will not engage you." She breathed a sigh of relief until Rytsar added, "In my circle, eye contact is a grave sign of disrespect and will be brutally punished."

Brie felt the panic start to rise again.

"But you will not fail in this," he stated firmly. "Even when we scene tonight, you will keep your gaze down at all times."

She squeaked out, "We're scening together?"

"Naturally, my comrades want to observe you at

play."

"What kind of scene?"

"One you're already familiar with," he assured her.

"But which one?" she pressed, frightened it might be his cat o' nines.

His lip curled into a seductive smile. "The cane."

Brie wasn't sure if a cane was any better than the cat o' nines in the hands of Rytsar. "I can still call out my safeword, can't I?"

"Of course, *radost moya*, but you will not. Tonight I'm going to teach you to enjoy the pain."

Brie trembled at the confidence behind his words. She had no doubt that she would be crying out in both passion and pain this evening. Although she feared what the Russian Dom had planned, the prospect of scening with him again was thrilling.

Rytsar smiled at her. "You are agreeable, then. That pleases me."

She felt the butterflies start. Why his praise had that kind of effect on her was a mystery, especially knowing his brand of kinky play. However, she had to silently thank Rytsar. By placing her in a new environment and setting up a challenging scene for her, he'd effectively sent Brie back to her training days.

It was strangely exhilarating to find herself in unknown territory again.

Savior

B rie was a bundle of nerves when they pulled up to an ancient stone building that looked suspiciously like a church, with its lone spire and stained glass windows lining each side. Had Brie been a simple tourist driving by, she would never have suspected that sadistic kinkiness happened within its majestic walls.

Rytsar helped her out of the vehicle with a devilish twinkle in his eye. "Are you ready to make me proud, *radost moya*?"

She smiled demurely, even though her entire body was buzzing with apprehension. She followed behind him at the required three-foot distance, while his entourage took their place behind her—a wall of protection she deeply appreciated.

Before they entered the building, Rytsar stopped and took off Brie's coat, grabbed the material of her bodice and pulled it down to expose her breasts. Her nipples instantly hardened, not liking the cold night air.

He smiled mischievously. "It's a requirement of the subs here."

Brie understood that nakedness was an effective method of humbling a sub, so she accepted the exposure with grace. She was determined not to draw attention to herself, but to keep her confidence nonetheless.

Rytsar used the huge iron knocker to announce their arrival, and the air reverberated with the deep sound of it as it shook the wooden door. A peephole immediately opened, and Brie dropped her gaze to the ground. Rytsar was asked a series of questions in Russian. After answering them, the heavy door swung open and he was invited inside.

The Russian Dom walked over the threshold without looking back. Brie's heart raced as she dutifully followed, staring hard at the heels of his boots. The conversation in the large gathering suddenly stopped, and Brie felt the heavy stare of everyone in the room as Rytsar spoke to the assembly.

Although she could only understand a few words, she did pick up Sir's name and 'American'. There were several manly grunts, then Rytsar strode to the back of the building. Brie struggled to keep up, disappointed that his men stayed behind, guarding the entrance. She suddenly felt vulnerable without them.

Keeping her eyes glued to Rytsar's boots, she still managed to catch glimpses of what was happening around her in her peripheral vision—there was a naked girl locked in a cage on the left, and a whipping pole with two scantily clad subs attached on the right.

From the sounds of the play, this environment was much rougher than anything she'd imagined. Brie's nipples hardened in fear when she heard a girl gagging as if being choked to within an inch of her life.

Yes, it was *much* darker play…

Rytsar strode up to an area in the back, where he stopped to talk to several men, leaving Brie free to observe covertly while she maintained her assigned stance.

To her immediate right, she saw the sweaty thighs of a woman. Her legs were spread wide and secured tightly with leather bindings. The sub was grunting from effort and discomfort as her Master slowly forced his fist inside her. Brie had never witnessed a fisting and found herself riveted to the spot.

It seemed crazy that people were engaged in normal conversation around her as this woman strained to take the unnatural girth of the man's large hand. Brie inched a fraction closer, wanting to get a better view.

She noticed the sub's pussy lips were glossy with lubricant, but stretched unbearably thin as her body tried to accommodate him. The woman lifted her hips, pushing against his hand in an attempt to break through her body's resistance.

He murmured low, nasty Russian words to the woman as he used a twisting motion to loosen her as he pushed farther in. Brie struggled to breathe as she watched his huge hand slowly disappear inside her pussy.

What does fisting feel like? she wondered.

Brie had never bothered to ask Mary, because she'd found the practice too kinky for her tastes, but being here and seeing it happen in front of her eyes suddenly had Brie curious.

The woman began tossing her head wildly, grunting

as the thickest part of his hand slipped all the way in, yet she never called her safeword. Brie assumed the scene was nearly over, but his hand continued its relentless progress until his wrist disappeared into her as well.

Brie swallowed hard when he started pumping his fist.

The woman's scream was muffled by a gag. Brie dared to glance up momentarily and saw that the sub's eyes had rolled back in her head. Brie looked back down at Rytsar's heels again, disturbed yet turned on by it.

The man did not slow down, mercilessly thrusting as the sub continued her muffled cries. It shouldn't have been sexy, but Brie felt wetness between her legs. The girl's willingness coupled with the man's ruthless desire was strangely arousing.

Brie could appreciate that when a sadist and a masochist got together, it was a fierce but sexually alluring dance.

She noticed Rytsar move away from the group of men and she obediently followed, still affected by the impassioned cries of the woman behind her. Rytsar led her to another section of the building, where a scene involving a stockade was in progress.

The sub was locked into the wooden device, but not in the normal kneeling position. She was facing upward in a pose much more difficult to hold. Brie instantly recognized the beauty of it for the Dom, because it left the sub's mound exposed for punishment.

"Higher and wider," the burly Russian barked. Brie was surprised to hear English and had to fight off the urge to look up. She wondered if he was doing it for her benefit, as Rytsar's guest.

She watched as the girl repositioned herself and lifted her pussy higher, her leg muscles straining with the effort. A flogger snapped across her bare mound, and the girl flinched. The strokes came faster and harder, reddening her pussy and thighs.

The sub's legs began to quiver as she forced herself to stay in place and take the wicked lashing. When her hips dropped just a fraction, he stopped and commanded her to reposition before starting up again.

If the sub's pussy hadn't been so wet, Brie would have considered his play too ruthless. However, she could not deny that the girl was not only taking her Master's punishment but enjoying it, based on the lustful expression on her face.

Rytsar had assured her that he would be able to train her to enjoy the pain. Brie shuddered as the flogger fell again, desperately hoping he was right.

There was a knock on the large door. After a short exchange, a new man wearing a superior smile entered, followed by his cowering sub. She removed his coat first and then hung up her thin shawl next to it, revealing that she was completely naked underneath. He led her to the center of the room by a leash and jerked roughly on the chain. She obediently fell to her knees.

He barked a command in Russian.

Those near her moved to allow the girl room as she listlessly leaned forward until her ass was in the air with her chin touching the stone floor. She grabbed her buttocks and pulled them apart to display herself to the men.

Rytsar's full attention was focused on the Master, not the girl. He stepped back and put his hand on Brie's shoulder and commanded, "Stay."

As Rytsar approached the new visitor, he asked warmly, "What do we have here?"

The man grinned. "I have a slave in need of a Master. Notice how tight it is." He pointed to the girl's sex. "Sewed it myself. Makes for a more satisfying claiming."

Rytsar stared at the girl's pussy as if he were genuinely interested. Brie squirmed, not caring for his interest in the girl. It was painfully obvious the sub was very young. However, it wasn't just her age that was disturbing. There was no expression of pride or joy on her face. The girl only conveyed resignation—and fear.

"Is she willingly compliant?" Rytsar asked.

The man stated proudly so everyone could hear his answer. "Oh, it obeys flawlessly. Would even die for me if I asked." As proof, he stepped on the girl's head, grinding her face into the stone floor.

The girl didn't move or make a sound, but when he pulled away she said, "Thank you, Master. Your pleasure is my pleasure."

Rytsar snorted, unimpressed. "Is she only motivated by fear?"

"This one has grown to love me over the past several weeks," the man declared, pulling on the leash. The girl stared up at him, her eyes communicating dread with a hint of longing.

Rytsar laughed amiably. "Survival instinct isn't love, idiot."

The man shrugged. "Who cares why it submits, as

long as it obeys every command impeccably?"

Brie gasped when the man kicked his submissive hard in the ribs. The girl only grunted, returning to her position. "Thank you, Master. Your pleasure is my pleasure."

The man smiled at Rytsar. "See? The perfect slave."

Rytsar walked around the girl, studying her carefully. "How long did it take to break her?"

"Wasn't much of a fighter. Not long."

Rytsar nodded as if he liked the answer. "So how much are you asking?"

The man's triumphant smile sickened Brie as he explained, "I had to travel a distance to attain it, and then there was the training..."

"How much?" Rytsar repeated.

"For you?" The man grinned confidently as he leaned forward and whispered in Rytsar's ear.

Upon hearing the price, Rytsar immediately snapped his fingers and one of his bodyguards came up, handing over a wallet stuffed with bills.

The girl's Master held out his hand, a condescending smirk on his face as he anticipated what looked to be a healthy payment.

"Before I conclude our transaction, tell me how you acquired the girl. I want to know her history."

"Simply an exchange student from Kazan."

"And her given name?"

"What does it matter?" the man scoffed.

"I'll pay you extra for the information."

The man pulled out a small notebook and flipped through the pages. "Stephanie."

The girl twitched but remained silent at his feet.

Rytsar stared down at her with a grave expression, then asked the man, "Do you feel any remorse for what you do?"

"What?" He laughed, looking at Rytsar as if he were joking. "I only provide what my comrades want." He glanced around at the women chained to equipment and huffed. "It's no different. I do not see victims in the world, only opportunities. If it's stupid enough to fall into my trap, it deserves its fate."

Rytsar's voice was deceptively pleasant when he said, "I agree, comrade. If you are foolish enough to walk into a trap, you deserve no mercy."

The man laughed, slapping Rytsar on the back. "*Da!*"

Rytsar handed the money back to his guard, looking down at the girl again. "I never play with a broken puppet. I find them disgusting, but the man who commands one is beneath contempt."

The man snorted angrily. "What do I care what you think? I have thousands who would pay good money."

"And each one is as vile as you."

"*Yeb vas,*" the man snarled. "I refuse to waste any more time with you." He called out to the others, "Who wants to bargain? You won't be disappointed by its service." He repeated himself in Russian when no one responded.

"A man without a soul endangers us all," Rytsar stated coldly.

Without warning, Rytsar hit the man with a sharp uppercut to the jaw, snapping his neck around severely. He crumpled to the floor like a ragdoll and did not move.

"No mercy," Rytsar spat as he walked away. He snapped his fingers, bloody from the impact, and two of his guards grabbed the man's arms and started dragging the lifeless body towards the entrance.

The tension in the room began to rise and angry murmurings began as the shock of what had just happened sank in. Rytsar faced them, his eyes flashing as he shouted to the crowd in his native language.

Rytsar turned to Brie, watching with satisfaction as his guards carted the man's prostrate body away. Under his breath he growled, "I refuse to condone human trafficking by standing idly by." He glanced at the cowering girl, still spreading herself out for the men.

"Kneel," he commanded as he walked up to her. The girl hesitantly got up from her display position and knelt at his feet, visibly shaking. He placed his hand on top of her head. "I am your protector. You are safe now."

She let out a tiny gasp as tears fell down her cheeks, but she dared not look up at him.

No one moved or spoke as the seconds passed, the gravity of the situation hanging over them like a dark cloud. When the two guards returned, the severity of their faces confirmed that the man was dead. Brie noticed that Titov held the man's notebook in his hand.

She shivered, unsettled that Rytsar wielded that kind of power. It made him far more dangerous.

He told Titov, "Look through the notebook. If you can't find what you need, call our contact in Kazan to find out who she is. I want her family contacted and their flight arranged. Also, ready my surgeon. Those stiches are to be removed when you reach Moscow."

Rytsar looked his men in the eye before instructing them. "I want both of you to go. Don't leave this one unattended—not for a second. They are fragile at this point."

"Understood," Titov answered gravely, picking up the whimpering girl from the ground and cradling her in his arms. Rytsar escorted them out, lightly touching the girl's forehead and whispering something to her before they left. The girl turned back to stare at Rytsar with a look of blind adoration as she was carried out.

After they were gone, Rytsar called Brie to him. Her heart raced as she approached the Dom, her eyes riveted to the ground. He grasped the back of her neck with the same bloodied hand that had just killed a man, sending spine-tingling chills through her.

"We are done here," he announced grimly.

The Dominants gathered around Rytsar and pounded their chests three times in unison. He nodded solemnly to them. Brie took it to mean what had happened would remain between them.

Once outside, Rytsar took a deep breath as he gazed up at the stars. Brie wondered what he was thinking, but was too shaken to speak. The remaining guard helped Brie with her coat and asked Rytsar, "Should I call for another vehicle?"

"No, we will walk," Rytsar replied, starting forward.

Brie knew the cabin was a fair distance away, and the night air below freezing, but she did not offer any complaints as she attempted to match his stride. His guard followed them at a distance.

Walking silently on the dark country roads of Russia with Rytsar beside her was surreal. Brie had just witnessed a side of the Dom she'd never seen—never known existed—and although she felt completely safe beside him, there was now an element of danger about him that frightened her.

After several miles, she finally found the courage to ask, "Do you think the girl will be okay, Rytsar?"

He acted as if he hadn't heard her. Instead of an answer, the crisp sound of their footsteps breaking through the icy snow filled the night air.

Eventually, however, he did speak. "It is a long, treacherous road. Some do not survive."

"Why not?"

He spat on the ground, snarling angrily under his breath, "They take their own lives, *radost moya*."

Rytsar's tone stopped any further conversation. Brie had never seen his dark and brooding side, and found it impenetrable. They walked the remainder of the trip in silence. She wondered about his past and how he knew of such things.

To keep from irritating him with further questions, Brie concentrated on the moon-bathed countryside, finding solace in the icy landscape. But when the warm light from the cabin cut through the trees, she squealed and started walking faster.

"Come, Rytsar," she encouraged, breaking into a run. She jogged the last hundred yards, arriving at the cabin coughing out the frigid night air that burned her lungs.

"That was foolish," Rytsar scolded as he walked up.

He helped her out of her coat and boots once they were safely inside. "Bathe to warm yourself," he ordered, smacking her hard on the ass as penance for her rashness. She was grateful to see a glimmer of the old Rytsar when she looked back at him.

Brie escaped into the bathroom and spent a long time soaking in the tub as she tried to come to terms with what had happened. It didn't seem real and she struggled to wrap her mind around the fact a man had been killed and a young girl rescued right in front of her very eyes...

After she'd toweled off and redressed, she went to find Rytsar, but stopped abruptly in the hallway.

The Russian Dom was seated in the main room, hunched over a single pillar candle as he lit it. His low voice drifted through the hallway as he whispered something over and over again while staring at the flame, lost in thought.

Brie understood it was a private ritual, and chose not to disturb him. Instead, she tiptoed to the bedroom and took refuge under the heavy blankets, still feeling unsettled by the evening's events.

Falling asleep proved impossible for her, but partway through the night Rytsar joined her. He pulled Brie to him with his strong, muscular arms and held her tight. His thoughts still seemed a million miles away, so Brie concentrated on slowing her breathing to help him relax. It took a while, but eventually his breath synced in time with hers, and soon after he was snoring quietly in her ear.

It brought tears to Brie's eyes when she heard it.

Whatever dark secrets Rytsar held, she would keep them safe. It was what Sir would want, and what her heart desired.

This Will Hurt

Brie woke up alone the next morning.

Rytsar's guard directed her outside when she asked where he was. She found Rytsar beside the cabin, chopping wood. He was silent, not addressing her even when she called out to him.

Taking the hint, Brie headed back inside, unsure what to do with herself. She was tempted to call Sir to ask for advice, but it proved unnecessary when the Russian Dom returned, noisily kicking the mud from his boots.

"Come here," he demanded in a gruff voice.

Brie quickly made her way over to him and automatically bowed at his feet because of the forceful tone of his command.

"Last night we were to scene together. That was taken from me. We will do it—now."

Brie looked up, a warm flush on her cheeks, remembering Sir's requirement of remaining true to herself. "You told me that you would make me enjoy the pain, but that frightens me, Rytsar."

For the first time since the incident, Rytsar broke into a smile. "Your fear is like sweet ambrosia to me."

Again, Brie was struck by the unsettling fact that her fear acted as an aphrodisiac.

"This will hurt, *radost moya.*"

He said it so casually, as if it were a romantic invitation.

"I'd be lying if I didn't admit I was scared to scene with you."

"Frightened but willing?"

Her heart raced when she answered, "Yes."

"Then undress and lie on the bed. I will get my tools."

Brie felt lightheaded as she slowly walked to the bedroom. It seemed unreal that she was about to give herself over to the Russian Dom.

She quickly stripped off her clothes and laid them in a neat pile on top of the nightstand before crawling onto the bed. Brie lay there, suddenly feeling naked and afraid. Goosebumps rose on her skin so she hugged herself, trying to keep her courage as she waited.

Rytsar did not hurry, purposely dragging out her anticipation—and dread.

Brie whimpered when he finally entered the room. She noticed that he was holding his hands behind his back so she could not see what he carried. The fact he was hiding it meant he was not going to use a cane for the scene.

Oh, hell, what did that mean for her?

"There are several things I expect from you during this session," he informed her. "First, you will be brave.

Second, you will be honest. Third, you will trust me."

Brie took a deep breath, sifting through her misgivings before she replied with conviction, "Yes, Rytsar."

He then surprised her by requesting, "What would you ask of me?"

She had to think for several moments before she came up with her answer. "I understand it will hurt, Rytsar, but I don't want to be permanently damaged physically *or* psychologically." She added with a hesitant smile, "I want to still like you when we're done."

"Hah! You will like me even more when we are finished, *radost moya*," he stated brazenly.

Rytsar laid his instruments on the dresser on the other side of the room, still keeping the items a mystery to her—all but one. He held up his Hitachi and raised an eyebrow. "This will open you up to enjoy my unique attention."

She licked her lips nervously and blurted the first thing that came to mind as he approached the bed. "I remember that you told me once that my body was like a child learning to walk and it needed your guidance."

He nodded slowly, a pleased expression on his face. "I'm impressed you remembered that. It's true. I can help change your body's response when it comes to the pain I inflict."

When the bed shifted with his weight, it suddenly became real to her so she asked another question, stalling for time. "Before we start, can I ask why you enjoy hurting people?"

He paused, tilting his head charmingly. "For me, it is the highest form of submission—relinquishing one's own instincts of self-preservation and self-gratification to satisfy the cravings of another. It is the ultimate power exchange, but means nothing unless it is given willingly. A sacred part of the person, a part they never share, is handed over to me in the exchange." He smiled lustfully at her. "I find it my drug of choice."

His words had a hypnotic effect on her. She longed to know the intimacy of that exchange and to share it with the man before her.

Rytsar turned on the Magic Wand and the familiar buzzing filled the room. "First, I reward your willingness." Rytsar placed the vibrator against her clit. She turned her head away, embarrassed by how quickly her pussy responded to the vibration.

"Eyes on me the entire session," he commanded.

She looked at him and lost herself in the intensity of his pale-blue gaze. Her first orgasm followed a short time later.

Rytsar pulled the wand away, telling her, "That is a good start." To her surprise, he placed it back on her clit and ordered, "This time you will come harder."

Brie often found it difficult to come consecutively, but forced her body to relax so that the sensation of the vibrator could take over and carry her on to another orgasm.

Rytsar was talented with the tool, watching her intently and pulling the wand back whenever her pussy started to pulsate with need. He was determined to build the second climax, and was highly skilled at the process, so in tune with her responses that it was as if she were guiding the wand herself.

Brie moaned when he pulled it away again, desperate to enjoy the aching release he'd produced with his tool.

"We are close," he assured her.

She nodded, relaxing her muscles and willing her thighs to stop shaking. When he placed it back on her clit, however, they started trembling again. Brie knew it was going to be a powerful orgasm.

"Come for me, *radost moya*."

Her eyes rolled back in her head as she let go and allowed her body to embrace the climax it had been fighting. Brie's hips lifted as her body came hard against the vibrating wand.

Rytsar murmured passionate words in his native tongue as she orgasmed for him, enhancing the experience and turning her on even more. Afterwards she lay there like a ragdoll, already spent, and they hadn't even begun yet.

"Now that we have your body primed, I will introduce you to the process."

Rytsar left her side and returned with a beautiful set of clover nipple clamps attached together with a heavy chain. She was familiar with them because she'd seen them used at clubs, but she had never experienced them herself because they were notorious for being extremely painful.

Brie looked at Rytsar fearfully.

"You know the bite of this clamp?" he asked.

"Only by reputation. I've never wanted to play with them."

"They *will* demand all your attention."

Brie looked at the clamps warily, whispering to herself, "I hope I can handle this…"

Rytsar grabbed her chin and stated in no uncertain terms, "You will be brave."

She faced his intense gaze and nodded.

Rytsar released his hold, laying the clamps on her stomach. She jumped and then giggled nervously, surprised by the chilliness of the metal.

He pulled a length of rope from his back pocket and bound her wrists together, securing them above her to the headboard. Then he began caressing her breasts with both of his large hands. "Your body is already flowing with endorphins. It's hungry."

She stiffened when he began pinching her left nipple, making it hard and erect. Brie knew he was readying it for the evil clamp, and starting breathing more rapidly.

"Yes, I want you to anticipate the pain."

Brie realized that Rytsar was the opposite of Tono Nosaka in a scene. Whereas Tono knew how to bring peace to her soul as he carried her along, Rytsar enjoyed the thrill of her fear and encouraged it.

Polar opposites with the same end goal.

She cried out when he picked up the clamp—before he even brought it anywhere near her poor nipple.

Rytsar's chuckle was low and charming as he grasped her breast with one hand, squeezing it so her nipple protruded while he opened the clamp and placed it on either side of her innocent nipple. She stared at it in dread, knowing he was about to let go.

"Look at me."

Brie looked up as he slowly released his hold on the clamp and it closed around her tender flesh. Her eyes widened as the pain registered, and she whimpered. She'd promised Rytsar she would be brave, so she silenced her cries, although tears formed as she fought through the sharp, throbbing ache it caused.

"I know your low tolerance for pain, *radost moya*," he murmured as he kissed her on the lips and then left a trail of fiery kisses down her throat to her other breast. "I appreciate the sacrifice of your will as you struggle to obey."

All Brie felt was the sharp pain of that clamp. It took over every thought but one as he pulled and pinched her other nipple.

Oh, God, he's going to do it again…

Brie felt the same wild terror she'd witnessed when filming his sub, as he picked up the attached clamp and dragged the chain across her skin, bringing it to her other nipple. She fought the urge to look and kept her gaze locked on him.

Rytsar's eyes shone with unbridled lust. She'd never seen him look at her that way before and it moved the submissive in her. She longed to please him—to be fully pleasing to him.

Knowing he valued her willingness, Brie forced herself to lift her right shoulder, offering her nipple to him even though everything inside her was screaming to push away.

The smile he bestowed on her was worth the sacrifice.

He lowered the clamp and released. Shooting pain erupted from the contact and she closed her eyes, trying to prevent the tears that now streamed down her face.

"Open."

She forced her eyes open, letting out soft mewing sounds as she struggled with the unbearable pain. "It hurts."

"I know."

The lustful confidence in his voice stirred her loins, and she felt a trickle of wetness. She looked up at the ceiling, doubting she could stand the pain for long.

"I want you to listen to my voice as you come, *radost moya*."

Brie was unsure if climax was even possible, but Rytsar had commanded her to trust him, so she nodded.

The pleasant buzzing of the Hitachi started up. She opened her legs wider when he placed his hand on her thigh.

"Concentrate on the vibration and my voice."

Brie's clit was sensitive since she had come twice already, but she didn't fight the toy as it pressed against her. Rytsar began murmuring to her in Russian, words she did not understand, but the tone of which was sensual and intimate.

She had been down this path before when she'd tasted Master Anderson's bullwhip. She'd been able to transform the pain into pleasure, but it had been for a brief moment, not with sustained stimulus like this.

Brie laid her head back on the pillow and focused on the vibration of the Hitachi, letting Rytsar's voice carry her as she gave in to the demanding toy. The tone of his voice changed as he sensed her impending orgasm. Instead of pulling the wand away, he pressed it harder against her, coaxing a greater climax.

For a brief moment she forgot about the nipple clamps as the rush of her orgasm crashed over her. Brie let out a long, satisfied moan, basking in the heated release.

"Very good," Rytsar complimented as he turned off the wand and laid it to the side.

She was still floating on the aftereffects of her climax when he reached up and lightly pulled on the chain.

Brie cried out in surprise as a shockwave of pain coursed through her body, all of her attention suddenly back on the clamps.

"These are cruel devices, *radost moya*. When I pull on them, they tighten." He gave another gentle yank and Brie about jumped out of her skin, reacting to the viciously sharp pain.

"Please don't, please don't do that again," she begged, squirming away from him.

"But I must."

"No, Rytsar," she pleaded. "I can't take any more!"

"You are brave," he assured her. He pulled on the chain with a little more force and all her resolve left.

"No more, no more," she cried, desperate for the pain to stop.

"You will come as I slowly pull them off."

"No, I can't!" she cried.

"But you will," he answered with confidence.

She started to panic and begged, "Please don't make me do this, Rytsar. Please!"

"Trust."

Brie choked down her protests. She had desired this experience with him, but now that it was real she wanted to run from it. She glanced down at her nipples, dark red from the tight squeeze that the clovers had on them. She was surprised how beautiful her breasts looked, bound by the cruel metal as her chest heaved from fear and pain.

With tears still falling, Brie looked up at Rytsar again and said, "I trust you."

He caressed her tear-stained cheek and kissed her tenderly on the lips. "*Radost moya.*"

He left the bed momentarily and returned with a shirt in his hand. "When training the mind, one needs to entice all the senses."

He laid the shirt over her eyes. Brie smiled, taking in a deep breath. It smelled of Sir.

Even as she lay struggling with the intense pain, she could appreciate the thought Rytsar had put into this scene. Her wrists were bound, which was something he knew brought her a sense of security. Her eyes being covered gave her a deeper sense of confidence. And now Sir surrounded her with his masculine scent. The pain remained as acute as ever, but mixed with it were these pleasant stimuli she could hold on to.

Rytsar pulled her legs down and lay on top of her, still fully clothed. The pressure of his chest resting against the clamps was excruciating, but she was soon distracted by his insistent tongue as he kissed her deeply.

The Russian was aroused on a level she had never experienced with him. It was almost as if his kisses sucked the life from her soul, and she was willing to be emptied completely.

The hardness of his cock pressed against her mound through his pants as Rytsar began biting her, leaving a trail of painful kisses down to her collar bone. He grabbed her throat with one hand and came back to her lips, his kisses aggressive and demanding as he ground his cock against her.

"Oh, Rytsar…" Brie panted, caught up in his ravenous desire.

"Are you ready?" he growled.

"Yes."

The Hitachi came back to life as he repositioned himself between her legs and pressed it against her swollen pussy.

"No matter how painful it becomes, know that the clovers will not break the skin."

Brie nodded in understanding, taking in deep breaths of Sir as she gave over her will to Rytsar, letting him have his way. He teased her cruelly with the Hitachi, bringing her to the edge only to whisk it away, making her crave the release he refused to give.

She knew he was waiting for her. Waiting until she couldn't take any more and begged for the pain.

"You are a fighter," he praised, "but I will not lose." He switched the wand to the higher setting.

"Mercy," Brie cried when it vibrated against her clit.

Rytsar chuckled under his breath, showing her none.

He's right, Brie thought as her body longed for release, *this is the ultimate power play.*

To experience release she had to submit to his pain, something she would never willingly do under normal circumstances. With her thighs quivering uncontrollably and her body covered in a sheen of sweat, she finally gave in to Rytsar's will.

"Please."

He began pulling on the clovers as he repositioned the Hitachi. The clamps squeezed like devilish vise grips as the raging fire below caught hold.

"Let it happen…"

The intense pain overwhelmed her and a terrified scream escaped her lips when he gave the clovers a final tug, ripping them from her body. In that moment of excruciating pain, she orgasmed with such delicious violence that everything went black.

She heard Rytsar's voice calling her name, but she wasn't ready to come back quite yet, still flying on the cloud of ecstasy he'd created. The Russian called her name again, lightly slapping her face.

With determination, she opened her eyes for him.

Rytsar shook his head as he wrapped his arms around her and nibbled on her shoulder. "Your Master mentioned your propensity to fly, *radost moya*, but I didn't realize you soar as deeply as some of my masochists."

Brie slowly floated down from her sub high, listening to Rytsar whisper to her in Russian in his husky voice. It was a beautiful way to come back to Earth.

She turned to face him and gazed into his pale blue eyes. Rytsar seemed unguarded in that moment. Ever since she'd first met the Russian he'd been daunting and mysterious, but now she saw a glimpse of the man behind the tough exterior.

He wiped away a remaining tear from her cheek.

"You were brave."

She glanced away, his praise unsettling—but in a good way.

Rytsar lifted her chin, forcing her to look at him. "I'm impressed."

Heat rose to her cheeks as she admitted quietly, "That pleases me."

He gazed into her eyes, saying nothing. It was an exchange unlike any she'd had with the Dom because it was intimate and real.

"I have known you from the beginning, when you were new and uncertain."

She giggled. "Yes, you have."

"You've grown since. Yet even then I understood my comrade's fascination with you."

"I'll never forget how you made my fantasy come true with such thoughtful accuracy, like a craftsman." Brie laughed to herself. "Of course, I found out you were a sadist months later. I felt kind of sorry for you."

"No need. Taking you so early in your training was a privilege."

"I was shocked when Sir told me that you were friends and that he'd specifically invited you to bid on me."

"We are brothers, he and I. The only person I trust."

Brie smiled sadly. "I'm sorry to hear that."

Rytsar stroked her cheek with his rough hand. "I do not trust easily, and yet I expect it from my subs."

"You are demanding, but you earn that trust."

"Trust begets trust. Therefore I will allow you one question."

In the Woods

"I can ask you anything?"

He nodded solemnly.

Brie looked into Rytsar's intense blue eyes. "What were you like as a child?"

He laughed. "I tell you to ask me anything and *that* is what you choose?"

She shrugged. "I always wonder that when I meet people."

Rytsar rubbed his bald head, a slight grin on his face. "I was precocious. My mother had her hands full."

"What was she like?"

"Only one question."

"But your mother is a part of your childhood," she protested.

He gave her an exasperated look, but his eyes shone with tenderness when he told her, "I would describe my mother as beautiful. Stunning in looks, but it was her passionate soul—and endless patience—that I remember most."

"Did you take more after her or your father?"

"So many questions," he growled.

"But still related to your childhood," she reminded him.

Rytsar frowned, but she noticed the twinkle in his eye when he answered, "The Durov line runs deep, obliterating any genes that cross with it."

"So you look like your father?"

"A spitting image of my father."

"He must be a handsome man, then."

Rytsar's eyes narrowed. "Are you flirting with me?"

Brie shook her head. "No, just stating the obvious."

"Hah!" he exclaimed, but she saw the flash of a smile. "My father was well known for his looks, but it was my mother who stole people's hearts."

"Then you *do* take after your mother."

"You are playing a dangerous game, *radost moya*." He laughed, then looked away, sighing. "I wish I could show you a picture of her, but the fire destroyed all my memories."

"Then describe her to me," Brie encouraged. "Help me see her in my mind."

"Ah, well, she had extraordinary pale gray eyes and playful arched eyebrows that could charm the bitterest man. Her high cheekbones complemented those soulful eyes, but it was her smile that bewitched and conquered all who met her."

"She sounds stunning."

"Her looks only hinted at the exquisite soul underneath." He looked at Brie with a serious expression. "But nothing could withstand my father's will, not even her. You see, a woman does not choose a Durov, she is chosen. Needless to say, when my father met my mother, her fate was sealed."

Rytsar abruptly changed the direction of the conversation. "If it weren't for her patience and understanding, I would be a different man, *radost moya*. Never underestimate the power you will have as a mother."

Brie blushed, embarrassed he was bringing up the prospect of her motherhood again.

"I have brothers," he told her. "Did you know that?"

Brie shook her head.

"*Da*, four of them."

"Wow, I can't even imagine." Brie was enchanted by the thought of there being four more Rytsars in the world, but wondered why she had never met them. Not wanting to lose this rare peek into his life, she said, "Your mother must have been an exceptional woman to raise so many strong-willed men."

"You will be too," Rytsar stated confidently. "I look forward to seeing you with your offspring."

"So where is she now?" Brie asked, secretly hoping he would offer to take to her to meet his mother.

"What has that got to do with my childhood? We're done."

"But—" She wasn't ready to give up her aftercare so soon and quickly changed tactics, laying her head on his muscular chest. "Thank you for guiding me through the scene, Rytsar."

A low rumble of satisfaction emanated from deep within his chest. "Now that you've made it to the other side, what are your thoughts?"

"It was an incredible rush, but equally frightening."

"Although I find your tears as charming as your smile," he murmured gently, "with a little patience I could condition your body so that you would come to anticipate my pleasure, not fear it."

Brie lifted her head from his chest and grinned. "Still determined to convert the non-masochist?"

He shrugged. "You are an itch I can't scratch."

She was shocked to hear those words coming from Rytsar. They were the exact ones Ms. Clark had used with her.

"What?" he asked when she stiffened.

Sir had warned Brie never to bring up Ms. Clark to Rytsar, so she quickly answered, "It's nothing."

Rytsar grasped the back of her neck and squeezed, demanding, "What's wrong?"

"I'm not allowed to talk about it," she explained.

"There are no secrets when it involves me," he said, becoming noticeably irate.

"Trust me. It's not worth repeating, Rytsar."

His grip became tighter. "No games, *radost moya*."

"Ms. Clark said the same thing once."

His tone became cold and guarded. "About me?"

"No, she said it to me off camera, during my documentary interview with her."

Rytsar growled. "Does your Master know what she said?"

"Of course."

"And he still lets you interact with her?"

"Yes, I saw her in Denver during my last visit…"

Brie was afraid to say more and stopped, for fear of upsetting him, but he wouldn't have it and demanded,

"Go on."

"She's working at Master Anderson's Training Center now."

He snarled, "I must talk to *moy droog*."

"Rytsar, Sir believes she's changed, and I would agree after seeing her this last time."

His nostrils flared. "She is not to be trusted, especially not with you. Just because he helped train her, Thane feels responsible, and that blinds him to the truth."

Brie wasn't sure if Rytsar was being overly protective, or if he perceived something Sir could not.

Rytsar asked in a deadly serious tone, "Do you trust her?"

She frowned. "No, not completely." But then she quickly added, "Still, I trust Sir's evaluation of her."

"I appreciate your loyalty, but I will be speaking to your Master when I see him today."

"What do you mean, *today*?"

"I called him this morning to collect you."

Brie was taken aback. "Why?" She was heartbroken to hear that her Russian trip was ending so soon.

"You cannot be associated with what happened last night. No one knows you are here other than my men and those at the club. They will not talk. However, I cannot risk your further exposure."

"So you really killed that man?" Brie asked in the barest of whispers.

"I killed no man, only a maggot."

Brie shuddered, remembering the cowering girl at the club. "I can't believe a person could treat another human being that way."

"The soulless don't have a place on this Earth."

She recalled the look the girl had given Rytsar as she was carried out of the club, and asked, "What did you say to the girl?"

He pulled Brie against him, smashing her face against his broad chest. "I told her that she was never a puppet, only a survivor."

Tears came to her eyes. After the horrors the young woman had experienced, Brie could only imagine how empowering those words must have been to her. "You're a good man, Rytsar."

"Enough," he growled, squeezing her tighter.

Rytsar ordered Brie to ready herself for Sir's return and then meet him outside next to the woodpile.

Knowing that her Master was coming, Brie pulled out all the stops. She took a long bath in scented oils, styling her hair and dressing in her sexiest outfit, even taking extra time applying her makeup.

When she met Rytsar out at the woodpile, he laughed at her. "All that extra primping was unnecessary. Now strip down to your snow boots and take out that fancy doodad in your hair."

"But it's cold," she protested, while still dutifully unzipping her skirt.

He pointed to a large tree and stated with amusement, "It's not cold in the sunlight, *radost moya.*"

Brie undressed, laying her clothes on a fallen log before placing her decorative comb on top. She stood beside the large tree he'd indicated, wearing nothing but her fur-lined boots. Her tender nipples hardened from the chill in the air.

"Much better," Rytsar praised, as he approached her with three long strands of leather in his hand.

She looked at him warily. "We aren't having another lesson on pain, are we?"

He laughed without answering, as he pressed her against the rough bark of the tree trunk and lifted her arms above her head. Rytsar secured her to the tree with the leather, tightening it firmly around her wrists.

The second one he wrapped around her torso, just above her mound. He kissed her on the lips as he cinched it tight. It was deliciously sexy, and she purred when he pulled away.

Rytsar smiled seductively as he instructed Brie to place her feet together, then knelt to bind them to the tree. He ran his hands over her body when he was done, starting from her bound ankles, over the swell of her womanly hips up to the curve of her breasts. Then he stepped back to admire her more critically.

"Yes, a very nice form to be greeted with," he stated, before moving back over to the woodpile. He started chopping again.

It was curious to be bound to a tree, completely naked in broad daylight, waiting for her Master's arrival. Brie looked at the birds in the trees above her and wondered if they found it equally odd.

Rytsar's remaining guard came out and spoke to him in Russian. As he turned to leave, the man glanced briefly at her. Although his overall expression did not change, she could have sworn she saw him lift his eyebrows as he walked by.

She looked back at Rytsar, who was wiping his brow of the sweat caused by the strenuous work. It seemed he was putting all of his unspent sexual energy into the act. When he put down the ax and took off his shirt, Brie was tempted to let out a whistle of appreciation.

He looked in her direction as if he could feel her admiration and nodded with a smirk on his lips before picking up the ax again to chop the next block of wood.

Brie studied his rippling muscles every time he swung the ax. The man was impressive in both form and confidence, as he precisely cut the wood into quarters and stacked them up.

She vividly remembered what he'd looked like when he'd been fucking the sub during her shoot in Moscow and shivered. Soon that would be her—with Sir.

Trinity

When Rytsar had cut all the wood, he slammed the ax into the chopping block and grabbed his shirt. He looked at her with a mischievous grin before walking into the cabin.

Brie couldn't believe that he was leaving her bound and alone in the woods. She looked around nervously, certain the Russian countryside had huge, fearsome bears. Suddenly the sounds of the forest became almost sinister as she imagined a giant Kodiak meandering through the woods, heading towards her.

"Rytsar," she called out. When she got no response, she yelled toward the cabin, "Rytsar, please don't leave me ou—"

It was then that she noticed he was standing by the window, silently watching her as he chugged down a glass of vodka.

Of course...

This was another experience he wanted her to have, to embrace, while he watched over her protectively.

Feeling his eyes still on her, she lifted her head,

standing up straighter so that she kept a long, lean line, while she pressed her shoulders against the tree so that her back arched slightly, thrusting her breasts forward.

If she was to be his bound captive, then she wanted to be the best-looking sub he'd ever tied to a tree. Brie closed her eyes and lifted her face towards the sunlight, relishing its warm caress on her skin.

She stayed in that position for what seemed like hours, fighting against the ache in her muscles as she listened and became connected with the nature around her. She secretly hoped that the two men would play with her outside. It would be exhilarating to know that kind of uninhibited freedom.

In the far-off distance she heard the faint rumbling of a car engine. Her heart rate increased.

Master is here!

What would he think when he found her here, bound outside in nothing but boots? Brie purred at the thought, her eyes glued to the vehicle when it rounded the bend. Sir got out of his car and looked her up and down with appraising eyes, but she was startled when he headed towards the cabin without saying a word to her.

She watched in disbelief as Rytsar opened the door and invited him in, leaving her outside—alone again.

A taste of objectification.

Brie looked at the cabin and felt butterflies when she saw both Rytsar and Sir watching her from the window. She could see their lips moving as they spoke to one another. Knowing they were talking about her as they admired her bound form was incredibly arousing.

The two came out a short time later, both shirtless

and holding tools in their hands. She wanted to squeal with happiness, tickled it *would* be an outside session with them.

Sir laid his assortment on the hood of his car and approached Brie with a dark purple flogger in his hand. Brie bit her bottom lip, anxious to feel its caress on her skin.

"Hello, téa."

"Good afternoon, Master."

"Did you miss your Master?"

"I did, very much! Although I was well cared-for."

"I'm glad to hear it." He ran his hands over her tender nipples and she cringed. "I see Durov worked you over this morning."

She agreed, "It was a very challenging session."

"But I heard you did well." He brushed her cheek with his free hand. "Always growing, always expanding your horizons..." Sir bent down and kissed her firmly on the lips, slipping his tongue inside her mouth. Brie groaned, lost in the sensuality of his kiss.

He pulled away and began swinging the flogger back and forth. "Because you have been good, I think you should be rewarded with a flogging."

"Thank you, Master." Brie gazed longingly at him, ready for the session to begin.

He moved her hair back before he started stroking her lightly on the stomach with the flogger, smacking the leather on one side and then the other in a fluid motion. Sir slowly started up her torso, caressing her skin with the multiple tails as he advanced towards her breasts. They bounced erotically when he reached them, sending shockwaves of pleasure to her loins.

Without missing a beat, he started back down, going past her hips down to her thighs. His lashes were becoming stronger, but remained pleasant as he warmed up her skin with the tool. Then Sir suddenly grabbed the tails and stopped.

"Rytsar?" he called.

The Russian came up from behind, holding a wooden crop with accents of black leather and a short tail of gray horsehair on the end. It was a beautiful tool in its own right and she was curious how it would feel.

"We use these on our horses," Rytsar informed her with an impish grin.

Rytsar started by tickling her with the instrument. Goosebumps rose on her skin, the light sensation of the horsehair almost too much to take. She squeaked as he brushed over her stomach and breasts, lightly tickling her forehead and lips, causing delicious tingles that traveled straight to her loins.

Rytsar moved even lower, grazing her mound with the unique tool. Brie moaned softly, liking its gentle caress. That was when he introduced her to the other characteristic of his unique crop, whipping it against her leg.

Brie squealed at the sting of the pretty whip and squirmed against the tree as he continued to lash her with it. Who would have known a tool could be so sugary-sweet and cruelly stinging? She continued to flinch and giggle as he flicked the crop across her skin.

Sir returned with his flogger and Rytsar respectfully stepped out of the way. Her Master swept away the lingering sting by replacing it with the pleasant thud of his sensual flogger, and she purred in delight.

"You like that, don't you, babygirl?"

"I do, Master."

The woods filled with the sound of leather against skin, of soft squeals and whimpers as she took the onslaught of his flogger. He played with different sensations, creating caresses that soothed and lashes that challenged, all the time keeping her enthralled and hungry for more.

Before he finished, Sir smiled at her wickedly. With quick, deft movements he lashed her sensitive nipples, first the right and then the left. Brie cried out in surprise, her tender nipples contracting achingly. He leaned over and licked them both before leaving her side, announcing, "I'm not done with you yet."

Sir retrieved something from the hood of his car and returned to her. She looked at his hand and shivered when she saw the small purple toy was partially made of ice.

"Your nipples look so sexy, all hard and pink. Let's see if we can make them even harder."

They were already so sore from her session with the clovers that Brie begged, "Please, no...Master."

Sir raised an eyebrow, shaking his head in disappointment. "I distinctly heard the word 'no' come from those sweet lips."

Brie realized her error and corrected herself, "I meant only if it pleases you, Master."

"That's what I thought you meant to say." He shrugged at Rytsar. "So, shall we see how hard we can make them?"

"*Da.*"

Brie couldn't breathe as the men descended on her. Rytsar grasped her throat and growled into her ear, "This is what happens to subs who say no."

Sir slid his hand between her legs. Brie struggled against her bonds when she felt the cold ice. The tool had little icy nodules on the end to add to the stimulation. And then…it started buzzing.

Rytsar kissed her hard as Sir rubbed the freezing-cold vibrator against her clit. Her poor nipples contracted into tight buds ripe for sucking. The men took notice and descended on her breasts at the same time, each taking a nipple into his mouth.

With Rytsar's hand still against her throat, Brie's cry was muted when the men began sucking on them. She pressed against the trunk of the tree, overcome by the conflicting sensations coursing through her body—the warmth of their mouths, the chill of the vibrator, the soreness of her nipples and the overwhelming knowledge that both men were going to take her.

Tears ran down her cheeks as the first chilly orgasm hit and her body surged with forbidden pleasure. The men pulled back and stared at her critically.

"First she says no and then she comes without permission," Sir remarked, sounding as if he was stunned.

"You have a very undisciplined sub, *moy droog.*"

"Apparently. Shall we see if we can make her come again?"

"Let's."

Brie shook her head, but Rytsar grasped her throat

again, tightening his hold until she offered no further resistance.

The ice-cold vibrator was applied to her clit, and she gasped when Sir turned it back on. The men studied her face while they lustfully squeezed and caressed her breasts, so when that first pulse hit, they both knew it.

Sir tsked. "She seems to have no self-control today. What did you do to her?"

"I made her fly."

Her Master looked at her with sympathy. "Have you been played with too much, téa?"

Brie shook her head vigorously. However, her pussy would not be denied and she came again.

Sir took the toy from her and examined the ice vibrator. He seemed amused. "The heat of your orgasms seems to have melted my instrument, téa."

"I'm sorry, Master."

"I'm impressed, but before we play with you further, you will have to be punished for your transgressions."

Sir undid the leather around her wrists while Rytsar released her ankles. The Russian Dom took the two strips of leather and walked over to the car. Sir stayed to undo the last one, around her torso. As he untied it, he told her, "I enjoyed driving up and seeing you bound, in nothing more than snow boots."

She smiled. "I enjoyed waiting for you, Master."

He led Brie to the car and told her to bend over the hood. She lay against it and glanced hesitantly at the leather straps as Rytsar handed one to Sir. They folded them over like belts and stood behind her on either side.

Brie looked at the reflection in the windshield and

held her breath as the two bare-chested Doms cocked their arms back to begin her punishment.

"Why are you being punished, téa?"

"I said no, instead of a proper submissive response."

"What else?"

"I came without permission, Master."

"Correct. Now take your punishment like the good girl you are."

Brie nodded, readying herself.

The two men worked as a team, starting on her ass and smacking her alternately as they moved down her legs with each strike. When they reached the sensitive area behind her knees, she cried out and bounced up and down on her tiptoes from the sting of it. They switched back up to the fleshy part of her ass again and started back down again. Brie hid the fact that she actually liked the feel of the leather and was super turned on by being the sole focus of these two extraordinary Doms.

Once Sir felt she'd been punished enough, he put down the leather strap and picked Brie up, slinging her nonchalantly over his shoulder. He headed towards the cabin with Rytsar following, staring at her like a hungry wolf.

The Russian Dom hadn't been able to satisfy himself with her earlier in the day, and looked determined to make up for it now. She glanced down and noticed just how ravenous he was.

"Yes, *radost moya*, that is for you."

She let out a little gasp and quickly looked at the ground, shivering with excitement. *Hell yeah, this session is going to be hot!*

Little did she know just how hot...

Sir set her down on the kitchen island and both men stood back to look at her while they talked. "I was thinking of starting with fire," he told Rytsar.

"Fine. You light her up while I partake of that generous mouth."

"Done."

While Sir readied the materials, Rytsar walked over to undo her boots, sliding them off and setting them on the floor. He then moved to her head, pulling her closer to him so that her head fell from the edge.

"She's never experienced fire play while giving oral sex," Sir commented as he dipped the large cotton swab into the alcohol.

Rytsar looked down at her. "Good. I like being a first."

Brie squeaked when the cold alcohol touched her skin. Her heart started beating faster in anticipation of the flames that would soon follow.

"Take her slowly so she doesn't move."

She heard the unzipping of pants and opened her lips when Rytsar brought his rigid cock to her mouth. Just as Sir had ordered, Rytsar was excruciatingly slow as he forced his shaft down her throat.

Brie moaned when the heat of the fire raced up the trail Sir had made between her breasts. Rytsar growled in response, liking the extra constriction it caused in her throat, as Sir tapped the flames out.

Sir dragged the swab against each thigh next, coming dangerously close to her bare mound. Rytsar pulled out to let her catch her breath momentarily, before slowly plunging back in.

Brie's muffled moan filled the kitchen when Sir lit each trail and allowed them to burn a little longer. After he'd swept the flames away, Rytsar held her head still, forcing the entirety of his shaft down her throat.

The rush of her heartbeat filled her ears as he kept her there.

Sir tapped the alcohol on each of her nipples and lit them on fire. She remained motionless, relishing the feel of heat on her nipples and the fullness of Rytsar's cock in her mouth.

This is what it means to trust and be owned. What a glorious feeling!

Sir cupped her breasts with both hands to put out the fire, while Rytsar pulled his shaft from her mouth. She gasped for oxygen, tears having formed in the effort.

"Color?" Sir asked.

"Green," she croaked. "I want more…"

Sir continued with the fire play while Rytsar fucked her mouth with excruciatingly unhurried strokes. She was in pure heaven, and it was evident from the wetness of her pussy when Sir slipped his hand between her legs.

He grunted his approval. "Why don't we try a real challenge? I'll bring her off while you come in her throat."

"*Da*," Rytsar said gruffly, his cock twitching as he pulled out, obviously liking the idea a little too much.

"Téa, you cannot move," Sir reminded her.

She lifted her head and nodded, desperate to meet his unusual challenge.

Placing the container of alcohol beside her, Sir

cleaned off his hands before moving between her legs. He gently slipped his fingers inside her moist pussy, then nodded to Rytsar.

Brie laid her head back and opened her lips for him. Just as the head of Rytsar's cock grazed the back of her throat, Sir's fingers began their magic. She struggled not to move as he quickly brought her to the edge.

Her whole body stiffened in response as she willed herself to remain still. Having come so many times already, she knew it was going to be quick and dirty. Brie moaned when she began to climax, feeling Rytsar's warm seed release in her throat, his cock pulsating with each burst.

That was when Sir encircled her bellybutton with a trail of alcohol and lit her on fire. With Herculean effort, she kept her hips from lifting as she came for them—fire, cock and pleasure her only reality.

Sir swiped away the flames with his free hand as Rytsar slowly pulled his spent shaft from her. She whimpered in pleasure, her pussy pulsing one last, glorious time around Sir's fingers.

"I love feeling you come, babygirl," Sir whispered huskily.

Brie pushed back her damp bangs, wiping the sweat from her face. "You are too much for me, Master—I love it."

Sir smiled to himself as he gently cleaned her skin, removing the residue left by their play. Meanwhile, Rytsar grabbed three glasses and filled them up with vodka. When Sir helped Brie off the counter after he was finished, Rytsar immediately handed them each one.

"To my comrade and his lovely submissive."

Brie lifted her glass and easily downed the smooth Russian vodka. She enjoyed the heat of the liquor as it went down, and mused that she was finally becoming a Russian at heart.

Sir led Brie to the couch and had her kneel at his feet while he played with her hair. He asked Rytsar to explain what had happened at the club. Afterwards, he questioned, "How is Titov handling it?"

Rytsar sucked in his breath, shaking his head. "It isn't easy, but this experience has been therapeutic—for both of us. If you cannot save the one you love, saving someone else is the next best thing."

Sir put his hand on his friend's shoulder. "So true."

"The girl has a strong spirit and was not in the hands of the maggot for long. There is hope it will not end like it did for Tatyana."

Brie wondered what the story was behind Tatyana and Titov, and how Rytsar was involved. She hoped Sir would shed some light on it later, when they were alone together.

"I don't expect any trouble, *moy droog*. No one will report that the maggot has gone missing, and the girl doesn't even realize he's dead."

"No chance Brie will be associated with this?"

"No. I kept her away from the girl, and my comrades at the club will never speak of it. It's as if it never happened." Rytsar glanced at Brie. "However, I don't like to take any chances with her."

Sir pulled her hair back to gaze into her eyes. "Are you doing okay after what happened?"

Brie licked her lips, still unsettled by the events from the night before. "I'm in shock, Sir, but grateful Rytsar did what he did."

"Unfortunately, it means we'll be heading out tonight. I was hoping to spend more time here at the cabin."

Rytsar stood up and put his hands on his hips, showing off his impressive chest muscles to Brie. "Since that is the case, I would like to sample more of your Brie, *moy droog.*"

Sir nodded and looked down at her. "Are you ready to be fucked, téa?"

The butterflies started as Sir stood up and offered his hand.

Brie trembled as she took it. "Please, Master."

They took her into the bedroom, where both men undressed before her. She swallowed hard, stunned by this rare chance to take in their handsome physiques. Sir, tall and striking, and Rytsar, all muscle and brawn—a girl's fantasy.

It was obvious the men had already talked about how it would play out, because Rytsar lay on the bed, stroking his cock as he watched her.

"Kiss me," Sir commanded.

Brie glided over to him, her body already aching with excitement. Standing on her tiptoes, she leaned up to kiss her Master. He took her face in his hands and kissed her hard, groaning as their tongues intermingled.

Oh, the taste and sound of Sir...

While they kissed, he took her hand and placed it on his hard cock. Brie moaned, loving the feel of his physical excitement. She lost herself in him, floating on an emotional and sexual high as she stroked his manhood.

Her manipulation proved pleasing, as Sir's cock became slippery with pre-come. Brie forgot herself in the joy of his tongue and cock, and started stroking him a little too vigorously. He abruptly grabbed her wrist.

"Too much," Sir growled, biting her on the shoulder as his cock pulsed in her hand.

Once he had successfully averted the orgasm, he gave her one more kiss and then pushed her towards the bed. "Please him, téa."

Brie moved with sensual grace, knowing both men's eyes were on her. She crawled onto the bed like a cat and straddled Rytsar.

"*Radost moya*, kiss your Russian."

Rytsar wrapped his muscular arms around her and kissed her fiercely, taking out his pent-up arousal on her lips. She met his kisses with equal passion, her pussy longing to be taken.

Lifting her waist while not giving up her lips, Rytsar pressed his cock against her wet opening, guiding her down onto his shaft. She opened her eyes and gazed into his pale blue eyes as she took his length. The connection was so powerful that her heart fluttered unexpectedly.

Sir came up from behind, lathering his cock generously with lubricant. He placed his hand on her ass and guided his cock to her tight hole, but once there he stopped.

"Look back at me."

Brie broke the kiss with Rytsar and turned back towards her Master. He swept her hair to the side so he could see her face clearly.

"There's my beautiful girl," he said soothingly, pressing his cock against her anus. "You have such a fine ass, my little sub." He ran his hands lightly over her flesh, which was still pink and tender from her punishment, before grasping her hips and pushing into her.

Both men groaned as the head of his shaft forced its way in. Sir grabbed her throat, kissing her as he rocked his hips, driving his cock deeper.

Brie had forgotten the challenge of taking two men at once and had to mentally relax in order to accommodate the fullness of them. It took several minutes, but once Sir was deep inside her, Rytsar wrapped his large hands around Brie's waist and began thrusting.

"Oh, yes," she purred, when Sir met those thrusts with alternating strokes.

Hearing the guttural grunts of both men as they took their pleasure in her was powerful, and Brie joined in the chorus—the three of them caught up in the erotic union.

Submissive bliss…

Soon, however, the men changed their focus, concentrating their efforts on rubbing her G-spot with their shafts at opposite angles as they stroked her in unison. It was too much stimulation, and she cried out for them to stop.

"Relax," Rytsar commanded, caressing her cheek.

Brie gazed into his eyes again. Did she trust them enough to give over control even when her body was violently fighting against it?

Yes.

She let out a long, drawn-out breath and consciously untensed her muscles, moaning loudly when they amped up their efforts again. Soon her breaths came in sharp, panting gasps as the overstimulation built a raging fire within her. Without warning, her body exploded in fierce, rhythmic waves as she gushed in watery release.

"Fuck, that was a good one," Sir commented, pulling out to look at her still-dripping pussy.

"Again," Rytsar demanded.

Brie whimpered as Sir plunged back into her and they started up again, increasing the tempo as they got her close to the edge. She threw back her head and screamed the second time her pussy rushed with her come.

She couldn't stop trembling after the second orgasm, her mind and body shocked by the intensity of it.

"One more time," Sir suggested.

"I can't…"

Rytsar insisted, "Once more."

This time they did not slowly build up the tempo, but started off fast and furious. The sound of skin against skin filled her ears, and Brie saw stars when she climaxed the third time, covering both men in her sweet-smelling come.

"Good girl," Sir praised, collecting her limp body in his arms and pressing her back against his chest. He nuzzled her neck and kissed her sweaty skin as Rytsar played with her breasts, pulling and tugging on her erect nipples.

"And now we will be gentle," Sir whispered gruffly.

He lightly pushed her back down onto Rytsar's chest

and the two began thrusting slowly. Their hands explored her body as they stroked her with their cocks, but they were so tender in their taking of her that it felt as if they were making love.

As Rytsar leaned up for a kiss, Brie was caught by the openness in his gaze. This was the man, not the sadist, who was being intimate with her. Sir lay down on top of Brie as the two men finished off, Rytsar biting her neck on the left as Sir bit her on the right. In that delicious moment, she felt both men come inside her.

It was then that Brie realized Sir had carefully orchestrated this intimate moment between them, and her heart overflowed with love.

A Call for Help

It was with regret that Sir and Brie left Rytsar at the cabin later that evening. As they pulled away, the Russian Dom pointed to the swing set.

Brie grinned while waving both her hands back and forth vigorously in a gesture of no.

"Why is there a swing set at the cabin?" Sir asked her.

Brie giggled. "Well, Sir, that's for the baby he thought we were having."

"Good Lord."

Brie threw Rytsar one last kiss, then snuggled up to Sir in contented silence as he drove them back to Moscow.

"I assume you want children," he stated later, as the city lights appeared on the horizon.

She looked up at him in surprise and smiled. "I do, Sir. When we're ready."

He let out a prolonged sigh, which frightened her a little.

"You want kids, don't you, Sir?"

He turned to her. "I'm not fit to be a father."

"Of course you are!" she assured him, squeezing Sir's arm in encouragement.

"Hell, Brie, I struggle enough with you. What child needs an emotionally distant father?"

"No parent is perfect, Sir, but you have a good heart. That's all a child needs."

He chuckled sadly. "If only it were that simple."

"I firmly believe a child created in love is blessed."

Sir shook his head. "Are you forgetting my mother?"

"No. I can never forget all that you've suffered. However, I'm selfish when it comes to you." Brie kissed Sir on the cheek. "If your parents hadn't fallen in love, I wouldn't be so deliriously happy now."

"To be honest, the idea of children scares me. It scares Durov too, which is why he wants us to have one so he can be an uncle, and not endure any of the complications of parenthood."

"Sir, I think it's normal to be unsure whether you'll be a fit parent or not. All we can do is strive not to repeat the mistakes of our parents, but hold on to the things they did right."

"So you've been thinking about this a lot, have you?"

She shook her head, giggling. "No, it was only Rytsar's incessant baby talk that had me pondering it."

"But you definitely want children."

"Yes." She laid her head on his shoulder, hearing the tension in his voice. "But not until you want to start a family. There's no reason to worry about it now."

Sir kissed the top of her head, saying nothing. Brie was still flying high from the day's events, and randomly burst out in a fit of giggles.

"What's so funny?"

"Oh, nothing. I just love everything about you, Sir."

While Sir finished up with his clients the next day, Brie packed for their long trip home. She looked around Rytsar's stylish apartment and sighed to herself. It was really a shame they had to leave so soon, but she was extremely grateful for what Rytsar had done.

Not many would risk themselves to help another, especially a defenseless girl. In her eyes Rytsar was a hero, but no one would ever know that except the girl, Titov and Brie.

Her thoughts were interrupted by the ringing of her cell phone. It was an unfamiliar number, so she picked it up hesitantly. "Hello?"

"Brie, is that you?"

"Yes." She couldn't recognize the woman's voice because it was so shaky with emotion. "What wrong?"

"They're kicking me out. They say I can't stay here anymore."

She was shocked when she realized it was Mary. "Who's kicking you out?"

"The commune! Master Gannon says I need..." Mary let out a painful sob, "professional help."

"Where are you now?"

"I'm still here, but he wants someone to get me as soon as possible." She started sobbing again. "I don't have anyone…so I called you."

Brie could hear how close to the edge she was, and took charge. "Mary, I'll talk to Sir and see if we can stop by to get you on our way home from Russia."

"How long will that be?" Mary cried.

"We're leaving today. I'll have Sir call Master Gannon once the arrangements are set. Trust me, we'll be there as soon as we can."

"Brie…I need Faelan."

Brie held back the tears, knowing that was not an option. "Don't worry, we'll be there soon."

Mary's voice was listless when she answered, "Okay…" Then she hung up.

Brie stared at her phone, stunned. It'd finally happened. Mary had hit rock-bottom. Brie desperately hoped they would be able to pick up the pieces.

She immediately called Sir and explained the situation.

"You call the airlines, while I find a suitable place for her to stay in LA."

"Sir, Mary's a mess. I don't think she can handle staying with strangers."

"I called Gallant about my concerns with Miss Wilson after we left the commune. He suggests Captain might be a viable option, should she need a safe haven."

"Yes! That's a perfect solution."

"It remains to be seen if Captain is up for such a challenge."

"But he likes Mary, and Candy is a survivor in her own right." For the first time since getting the call, Brie felt a glimmer of hope. "Thank you, Sir."

"The Center always looks after its graduates," he stated with compassion. She heard some men talking in the background and Sir said, "Look, I need to finish up here. Are you done packing?"

"Almost, Sir."

"Don't pack my extra belt."

Brie smiled to herself, suddenly anticipating the long flight home.

She spent the rest of the afternoon going over her footage from both Montana and Russia, having no doubt that Mr. Holloway would be pleased.

However, her mind kept drifting back to Sir. He'd explained to her father that he enjoyed tweaking the details of her life.

Well, that man tweaked them in the most delicious ways...

Pieces

Brie arrived at the Sanctuary with Sir just as the sun was setting. It had been a long flight from Russia, full of delays and unexpected layovers. Both were exhausted, but Brie felt her nerves hit when they drove up to the rusty gate. What would Mary be like, and could Brie handle her, given her current mental state?

The intercom crackled to life, and the rickety gate opened as soon as Sir stated his name. "Park your car and make your way to Master Gannon in his office, Sir Davis. He's expecting you."

"What about Miss Wilson?"

"She's with him now."

Sir drove directly to the main building, where they found Rajah waiting for them. "Please follow me," he instructed, glancing at Brie briefly with a look of concern. She picked up her pace, troubled by his unease.

Master Gannon greeted them at the door and ushered the two into his office. Mary was looking out of the window, sitting on a chair, curled up in a protective ball.

As soon as Brie saw her, she called out, "It's okay,

Mary. We're here now."

She slowly turned to Brie, a look of desolation on her face. Brie raced to her, and was surprised when Mary offered no resistance to the hug she gave her.

"What happened?" Sir asked Master Gannon as he sat down next to the girls.

He took his time to answer. "The community has endured several incidents with Miss Wilson, which leads me to conclude professional counseling is necessary."

Mary buried her head in Brie's chest.

"What was the nature of the incidents?" Sir asked.

"On numerous occasions she hassled and threatened one of our newest members, at one point even assaulting the man."

Sir turned to Mary. "Is this true?"

With her head still buried in Brie's chest, Mary nodded.

"Why, Miss Wilson?"

Mary did not answer Sir's question, choosing to remain silent.

Sir addressed Master Gannon again. "I'm sorry to hear that one of our graduates has behaved in such an intolerable manner, but I wonder if she was provoked."

"He was apprised of Miss Wilson's instability, and immediately stopped all private contact with her. We wanted her to succeed here, Sir Davis. I even took her under my wing once Mr. Wallace left, but Miss Wilson has become unruly, and the entire commune has suffered her irrational rants. It wasn't until she became physically violent that I made the decision to dismiss her."

Sir nodded.

"Unfortunately, this problem is much bigger than we can address here at the commune. I'm sure you agree that she needs professional help and I cannot further compromise the wellbeing of the community."

Mary groaned into Brie's chest.

"We will see that she gets the professional help she requires," Sir assured him.

Master Gannon called to her in an authoritative tone, "Mary."

She pulled away from Brie to face him, answering meekly, "Yes, Master Gannon."

"Although you are being sent away, you are important to this community. You will be welcomed back, should you want to return, but only after your counselor deems you fit and you have a partner who can join you."

Mary sucked in the sob that looked ready to burst forth, and nodded to him.

"All of her belongings have been set beside your vehicle," Master Gannon informed Sir. "I think it's best that you leave now. The sooner Miss Wilson starts on the road to recovery, the sooner she can move forward with her life."

"Agreed." Sir stood and took his outstretched hand. "Thank you for your care in this matter, Gannon."

Mary was slow to stand up, but quietly followed Sir out. While he put her luggage in the trunk, Brie was visited by Shadow. The cat rubbed against her leg, letting out a single meow.

She bent down to pet him, whispering, "It's good to see you too, my friend."

The cat sauntered back to its master, who stood

watching the encounter from the porch. "I was told that Shadow had an affinity for you, Miss Bennett."

Brie smiled up at Master Gannon. "He was a great comfort to me while I was here."

He stooped down and picked up the large black cat, cradling it in his arms. "I'm convinced he is an old soul with exceptional intelligence."

"I don't doubt it. I got the distinct feeling he could read my mind."

Master Gannon chuckled. "I feel that way myself at times. The fact that he comes to you when he is skittish around everyone but me, I find utterly fascinating." He scratched the cat's chin. It looked up at him, closing its eyes in blissful pleasure. The strong bond between the two was easy to see. "There are times when I wish he could speak, but I suspect it would lessen our connection."

"I can appreciate that," she agreed.

When Sir slammed the trunk shut, Brie headed towards the passenger-side door, but Mary stopped her. "Sit in back with me. I don't want to be alone."

Sir nodded his approval.

After saying their goodbyes to Master Gannon, the two women piled into the back seat. "Make sure you're both buckled in," Sir ordered as he slid into the front seat and started the engine.

Mary dutifully snapped on the belt, but slipped the shoulder strap behind her so she could curl up and lay her head on Brie's lap. It reminded Brie of the night at the Center when Mary had suffered a trigger while scening with Tono, which had left her an emotional wreck.

Brie stroked her long, blonde hair, knowing what a comfort it was when Sir did it to her. The drive to the airport was uneventful and quiet, almost peaceful.

Sir informed Mary, "You will be staying at Captain's home. Dr. Reinstrum has agreed to begin counseling you again, since he's familiar with your situation and feels he can help."

Mary only grunted in response.

"If you have any objections, you can stay wherever you wish."

Mary said nothing. Brie stopped petting her head and was surprised when Mary quietly pleaded, "Don't stop, Brie."

Brie looked at Sir in the rearview mirror, worried about the girl. This wasn't the Mary she knew. It was as if the life had been sucked out of her.

It wasn't until the airplane was on its final descent into LA that Mary began acting more like her old self and shared some of what had happened with her.

"After you left, I kind of lost it, I guess. God, I needed Razor to take the pain away, but the asshole refused. He avoided me like the plague—like I wasn't worth his time anymore."

"You know that's not true. He was instructed to leave you alone."

She rolled her eyes at Brie, growling. "All I know is how it made me feel...still makes me feel."

"They were only trying to protect you."

Mary snarled in disgust. "The fact that Faelan could just abandon me like that... What the fuck?"

"Don't even go there, Mary," Brie warned. "You disobeyed his direct order and were insolent when he called you on it. I'll never forget the look on his face."

"Don't," Mary snapped, tears forming in her eyes.

Brie took solace that Mary was showing some emotion at least. "You're lucky."

"I'd sure like to know the fuck how," she growled.

"You've got the entire Training Center behind you."

Mary pressed her forehead against the airplane window and said in a defeated voice, "You don't understand. Sometimes a person can be so fucked up there's no coming back…"

"The trainers believe in you. Captain does too. You're not alone, woman."

"What about Faelan?" Mary asked.

Brie hated to be the one to break it to her, but it had to be done. "You have to face the fact that his journey is no longer part of yours."

She turned to Brie, her stoic expression crumbling as she started to sob. Brie wrapped her arm around her and murmured softly, "Shh…shh…"

The people around them started to get visibly uncomfortable as Mary's sobs became louder.

"Miss Wilson," Sir said quietly from the seat behind them. "Although there is a time and a place for tears, now is not one of them."

Mary nodded, taking a deep breath before accepting the tissues he handed her. Brie looked back at Sir, at a loss for how to comfort her friend.

It was a helpless feeling.

Sir wasted no time getting Mary into the hands of Captain, driving straight to his home from the airport. Candy greeted them at the door with a welcoming smile. "Please come in, Sir! It's wonderful to see all of you again."

She took Mary's hands and squeezed them. "You especially, Mary."

Candy guided them into the sitting room, where Captain was waiting. Brie was shocked to see a collar in his hand.

"Before I allow you into my home, Miss Wilson, I insist you wear a protection collar. By accepting it, you are agreeing to follow my house rules, and I am agreeing to care for and protect you. I will only warn you once if you break any of my commands. A second infraction will garner swift punishment, and a third will be cause for dismissal. I do not tolerate disrespect in my home."

Mary looked at him in disbelief as she stared at the collar, but regained enough composure to ask, "What are the house rules?"

"You will not leave this house without my permission, you will perform duties to keep this household running smoothly, you are to remain in my presence at all times unless I command otherwise, *and* you will show the utmost respect to my submissive and myself. Do you understand?"

"I do."

"Do you agree to live under these rules?"

Mary looked apprehensively at Brie.

Brie understood how hard this was for her, and was relieved when Mary answered with a quiet, "Yes."

"Then kneel at my feet and accept this collar."

Brie held her breath as she watched Mary slowly kneel. The girl had never worn a collar—claimed she couldn't stand them—and yet there she was, kneeling at Captain's feet to receive the one he offered.

Captain looked down at her with sympathy, and in that moment Brie thought he was truly the handsomest man on Earth. After he'd fastened the black leather collar around her neck, he put his hand on her head. "Until the day I remove this collar, you are under my protection and care. You are to address me as Vader for the duration of your stay."

Mary gave him a questioning look. "Why?"

"My heritage is Dutch. As I am head of this house and caretaker to you, it is fitting you should address me as father."

The significance of the moment was not lost on Brie. Captain was taking on that role in Mary's life so he could help her to replace the cruel memories of her past with new, healthier ones. However, Brie was stunned to see tears streaming down Mary's face when she lifted her head and said in the barest of whispers, "Thank you, Vader."

Captain spoke to Sir. "Thank you for delivering her to me. My pet and I look forward to aiding in her re-education."

"Dr. Reinstrum will call you soon to set up her counseling sessions."

"I've already contacted him and it has been arranged."

"Perfect."

"Since you've had a long day, why don't you head home? She will be fine here."

Before Sir agreed, he asked Mary, "Miss Wilson, are you comfortable with us leaving?"

She wiped the tears from her eyes. "Yes. I am, Sir."

"You understand the rare privilege Captain has bestowed on you. I expect you to take full advantage of this opportunity for growth."

Captain placed his hand back on Mary's head. "Between my pet and I, I'm confident we can help her to overcome the barriers that hold her back."

Candy looked up lovingly at Captain. "My Master has a very big heart."

With his hand still on Mary's head, Captain cradled Candy's chin. "You are a pleasure to spoil, pet." He kissed her gently, fingering the collar around her neck.

It was a romantic scene that melted Brie's heart. Yes, there was hope for Mary in this home. Captain was a stern Dom and would not put up with her insolence, while Candy understood the pain of abuse. Together, they could prove to be exactly what Mary needed.

"Pet, you may tell your friend goodbye."

Candy walked over and hugged Brie. "It's so good to see you again. I hope we'll see more of each other from now on."

"Me too, Candy."

Captain looked down at Mary. "*You*, I need to think of a name for." He stared down at her for several moments and said with finality, "Your name will be *lief* in my home."

"What does it mean, Vader?" Mary asked.

"Before I answer, I want you to tell me what you think it means."

She blushed with humiliation when she answered. "Lost?"

He shook his head, smiling kindly at her. "I thought you might say something like that, but you would be wrong. It means well-behaved child. Now, *lief*, say goodbye to your good friend."

Captain lifted his hand from her head and Mary rocked on her heels and stood. The expression on her face was a mixture of relief and fear as she approached Brie.

Brie could appreciate her concerns. Captain had placed the burden of extremely high expectations on Mary, and the girl was unsure she could meet them. Brie whispered in her ear, "It's going to be okay. You're home."

Mary gasped softly, only nodding in response.

Brie had never seen Blonde Nemesis like this before—humble, weak and vulnerable. It was actually endearing, and made her want to hug the crap out of Mary. She surprised Brie even further when she didn't resist the embrace, resting her chin on Brie's shoulder and hugging her back.

Brie closed her eyes and smiled, filled with a sense of real hope.

Ice Goddess

It was wonderful to return to their own apartment. Brie had missed its familiar smells.

"Undress," Sir commanded as soon as he'd shut the door.

She was delighted to shed her clothes, all except the belt she'd worn the entire trip. She had forgotten about it after picking up Mary, but was very much aware of it now as she presented herself to Sir, kneeling at his feet.

"It's good to be home," he said, sighing with contentment as he lightly touched her head. "Stand and serve your Master, téa."

Brie stood before him, purring when he caressed her cheek.

"I have teased you, but now the time has come to satisfy you," he stated as he pulled on the belt around her waist.

"I've been looking forward to this moment ever since we boarded the plane in Russia," she confessed as they strolled down the hall together.

Once they reached the bedroom, he ordered, "Stand

behind the bed, legs spread, hands behind your back."

A few minutes ago, Brie had been ready to collapse on her Master's bed and fall asleep. Now she was staring at it with tingles of anticipation coursing through her body.

"I like having an array of familiar instruments at my fingertips," Sir called out as he scavenged through his tools in the closet.

"I like it too, Master."

She grinned when she heard his low, manly laughter.

Sir returned with a spreader bar, leather cuffs, and a bundle of rope, which he laid on the bed before her. He lit a single candle on the nightstand and took off his shirt, exposing his handsome chest covered in dark hair with the lowercase 't' resting prominently over his heart. The sight of him was swoon-worthy.

With tenderness, he placed the leather cuffs on her wrists, making sure they were tight, then attached them to the spreader bar. "Lift your arms," he commanded huskily.

This was new for her. Normally Sir used the spreader bar on her legs. She lifted her arms above her head and he took the rope, tying it to the bar. Then he strung the rope through a ring above her head and pulled it tight.

"Oh!" she gasped, liking the feel of the restraint.

"Keep your legs spread," he commanded as he pulled it tighter, causing her to tiptoe for him. He finished off the knot and stood back to admire her.

"Wait…"

He riffled through their luggage and produced her fur-lined snow boots. "I liked seeing you in these." He slipped them on and laced them up. "There. Now you look the part of my sexy ice goddess."

She basked in his gaze, her stomach fluttering as his hands traveled over her body, purposely avoiding her most sensitive areas and driving her wild because of it.

How was it possible, after all this time, that she still reacted so intensely to his touch? Brie never imagined that love could be this tangible and real—a part of her being. This wasn't lust that would dull over time; this was a penetrating love that now defined her.

"I love you, Master…"

"I love you, téa." Sir turned her head to face him and kissed her passionately on the lips. She swayed in his embrace, losing her balance but completely supported by her bindings—a willing but helpless plaything for her Master.

Sir took full advantage of her helplessness, telling her, "There's one more thing needed to make this scene complete."

He left her side and she listened to his echoing footsteps as he walked out of the room and down the hall. Brie shivered in expectation, wondering what surprise he had for her when she heard his footsteps return.

Sir pressed his body against her back, leaning forward to lightly nibble on her ear. "You're so hot, téa."

She shrieked when she felt ice against her clit and automatically clamped her legs shut, trying to protect herself from the cold.

"Tsk, tsk…"

"I was surprised, Master," Brie explained. "I'm sorry." With determination, Brie repositioned herself, leaving her legs wide open to suffer his wicked attention.

"Did you like Rytsar's ice vibrator?" he asked, pressing the ice against her pussy. "I could always order one for the closet."

Brie panted, forcing herself not to move even though her body violently resisted the spine-tingling chill the ice caused. "I prefer a hard cock and hot come, Master."

Sir chuckled in her ear as he slowly forced the half-moon of ice deep inside her. "Close your legs, téa. Let it melt. I plan to thoroughly fuck my ice goddess."

Brie looked upwards, biting her lip as she crossed her legs together, keeping the ice from slipping out as it chilled her from the inside. Her nipples became hard while goosebumps rose on her skin. Sir took notice and started tugging on her pert nipples.

She leaned her head back, hanging from the bar and moaning as water dripped from her pussy onto the floor.

"You like having your nipples played with."

Brie moaned louder as he rolled them between his fingers and answered, "You know how to send an electrical current straight to my sweet spot, Master. I'm desperate for you, even though I hate the cold."

"I, on the other hand, am anticipating it. Your chilled pussy is going to take a pounding."

More of the water spilled out in response to his words.

Sir played with the rope, loosening it so she was left bent over the bed but not quite touching it. He secured the rope again and stood behind her. "Seeing you bent over like this is such a turn-on, téa. Your perfect ass displayed and your pussy dripping for me."

Brie purred as the last of the melting ice trickled to the floor.

Sir moved into position behind her and fisted her hair, pulling Brie's head back. "Grab on to the bar and prepare to be royally fucked."

Brie wrapped her cuffed hands around the bar for greater support and closed her eyes when Sir grabbed her waist with his other hand, using it for leverage. He waited, building up the anticipation before plowing his hard cock into her.

The warmth of his shaft shattered the icy cold and Brie cried out in pleasure.

Sir's groan was low and primal, stirring the flames of her desire. Bound as she was, their movement was not hindered by friction from the bed, and she rocked into him with every thrust. He pulled her head back farther as he ramped up the pace, and soon the thrusts came so hard and fast that Brie felt the flutterings of subspace.

Sir suddenly pulled out and let go of her hair. Brie whimpered in protest.

"Come for me," he ordered, slipping his finger inside and simply resting it against her G-spot. His energetic thrusting had made her hyper-sensitive, and that simple pressure caused her to come around his finger. She let go of the bar and lost herself in the intensity of it.

"Good. I'm going to fuck you again. Hold on to the bar."

Brie grabbed the bar as he took her hips with both hands and pounded her with much greater force. Sir's breath came in short, raspy grunts from sheer effort as he gave it everything he had.

Brie began screaming nonsensical words as she took the onslaught, loving the carnal brutality of it. Never wanting it to end…

Sir stopped again, and with quick movements he untied the rope, lowering her onto the bed, his cock still buried inside her. Sir pressed the full weight of his body against her as he came. Brie moaned, feeling his cock pulse with each powerful release.

Her eyes fluttered closed and she came for him—again.

"Get your ass over here. I have to get out of this place now!" Mary screamed into the phone. It hadn't even been twenty-four hours, but she was already begging to leave.

"What happened? Did Captain hurt you?" Brie asked, genuinely concerned.

Her question grabbed Sir's attention and he stopped working to listen.

"Yes, I have been forever scarred by what I have seen. It was totally gross!"

Brie looked over at Sir, shrugging to let him know it wasn't serious. "What happened exactly?"

"Those two…together…they're horrifyingly cute, in a sickening way that makes me want to puke."

"What did you see?"

"Oh, my God! Here he is, this badass Dom, and he's petting Candy all the time, telling her how pretty she is and spoiling the bitch with little treats."

Brie couldn't believe Mary was being so rude and disrespectful of both Captain and Candy. "What the hell is your problem, Mary? You have no right to judge them!"

"Forgive me. I forgot I was talking to the biggest cheeseball of them all. Of course you would defend their behavior."

"Here I thought something serious had happened, and you're crying uncle because they're being sweet to each other?"

"It's disgusting, damn it! And he makes me sit in the corner and watch."

"What? Watch them having sex?"

"Hell, no. I could handle that. Instead, I'm forced to observe while he feeds her little bites from his plate, strokes her hair whenever they watch TV and kisses her goodnight before he chains her to the bed. OMG, it's more than any sane person can take."

"Before you say another word, answer me this. Has Captain mistreated you in any way?"

"Other than scarring me for life?"

Brie was not amused.

"He's been a complete gentleman—too much of a gentleman for my tastes."

"Why the heck are you calling me, then?" Brie asked. "You *do* realize how lucky you are that they took you in, right? You should go to Captain right now and bow at his feet. Thank him for taking in such an unworthy, sniveling worm."

"Shut up, Brie. You're such a fucking asshole!"

"You're the one out of line here, bitch. Anytime *anyone* shows you a lick of kindness, you stomp all over them like they did something wrong." Brie was shaking with repressed anger and growled, "I still can't get over what you did to Todd."

"What *I* did?!"

"Yes. You disobeyed a direct order, one he only had in place for your sake—and yet, before he left, he told me to take care of you. Even after all the shit you put him through."

"Oh, boo hoo… What else did he tell you?" she demanded.

"He said he was leaving the commune, but refused to tell me where he was headed."

"Hah!" Mary grumbled. "I don't fucking believe you. Yeah, I bet the two of you had a grand old time going over a long laundry list of my faults."

"You're a real piece of work, you know that? You don't deserve him, Mary. All Todd ever did was put your needs above his, and all you can do is bitch about him."

Sir took the phone from Brie. "Miss Wilson, this conversation has gotten out of hand. Is Captain treating you well? Fine, then show him the respect he deserves and don't call here again until you have learned something worth sharing."

Sir handed Brie the phone back with a disappointed look on his face.

"She just gets me so riled sometimes," Brie complained.

"With Miss Wilson, you must tread lightly. She already feels worthless, which explains her defensive tactics. When you tell her things such as she doesn't deserve Mr. Wallace, you only feed into her fears of worthlessness. Is that what you intended?"

Brie frowned. "No, but I just want her to admit she's wrong to treat people that way."

"I chose Captain to watch over her because of his background. He won't be swayed by her outbursts. Let the man do his job without undermining his efforts."

She hated that she'd made a mess of things, and bowed at his feet. "I'm sorry, Sir."

"Look at me," Sir commanded.

Brie looked up hesitantly, her lip trembling.

"I understand your anger towards Miss Wilson. She's been disrespectful to your friends and you felt the need to lash out. What she needs, however, is something you can't provide. Step back and let Miss Wilson work through her issues under Captain's guidance. Don't answer the phone if she calls again. She's been instructed to call me if she's being mistreated."

"Yes, Sir."

"Rather than worrying about Miss Wilson, I want you to unpack our things while you concentrate your thoughts on tonight's outing."

She looked at him questioningly. Sir answered that look with a smile, telling her, "I'm taking you to The Haven, my dear. And I have wicked plans for you." Sir held out his hand and helped her back to her feet.

It was like magic.

Like the night before, Sir had completely changed her mindset within a matter of seconds. Brie had expected to putter around for the next few days, recovering from their weeks of travel. Instead, Sir had them moving on with life, headed in a most delightful direction.

Triggers

Brie hadn't visited The Haven in over two months. She was excited at the prospect of seeing old friends and meeting new members who'd joined recently. The club had seen a significant influx in membership after the documentary, and had become the happening place in LA for kinksters.

She glanced at the mirror as she dressed in the vinyl outfit Sir had gifted her. The top was a sexy combination of a black corset with laces up the front and a hood in the back, attached to a high-low skirt that flowed like a long cape. The bottoms of the outfit consisted of simple short shorts, which were scandalously tiny. She felt like a vinyl priestess when she put it on, and twirled several times to admire the flow of the skirt. The outfit was outside Sir's normal tastes, but she liked it very much.

When Brie emerged from the bedroom, Sir let out a long whistle. "That looks killer on you, babygirl."

After twirling for him, she gushed, "Thank you, Master. I love it."

He held out his hand and she took it, standing gracefully before him. "My pleasure, téa. I like showing off my sub. Others can look, but they can't touch."

"Will we be scening tonight, Sir?"

"Yes," he said with a smirk, "I thought a little violet wand might add some spark to the evening."

She grinned. "Not only are you a talented Master, but a skilled comedian as well."

He swatted her butt. "Sarcasm will only get you in trouble, my dear. Expect to pay for that."

"I'm unsure whether to be excited or frightened."

The lack of amusement on his face made her heart skip a beat. Maybe she would pay dearly for her jest… It was the not knowing that thrilled her. Oh, how she loved his devilish humor!

Sir seemed to be in a particularly playful mood, and drove the car with gusto, taking sharp corners and punching the gas so that she was thrown back in her seat. Brie giggled for the entire ride, enjoying his expertise behind the wheel. She caressed the dashboard lovingly after he screeched to a halt once they reached The Haven's parking lot, appreciating the wildness the car brought out in him.

Brie waited for him to help her out of the car once he'd grabbed the duffel bag from the back. She walked confidently beside him, grateful that The Haven was nothing like Rytsar's club. She didn't have to worry about breaking some simple protocol and suffering punishment in front of everyone. Although Sir would certainly call her on a breach of protocol, *no one* would ever be allowed to touch her, much less punish her, without his permission.

She was surprised at the long line to get into the club, and stunned by the sheer number of people once they finally made their way in. The middle area was standing room only. It had the feel of a concert venue rather than a kinkster gathering.

Trying to make it to one of the alcoves proved challenging as Sir forced his way through the crowded room. Instead of taking Brie to watch a scene, he went directly to the club's owner.

"Is it normally like this, these days?" Sir asked.

"Fridays and Saturdays are the worst. If you want a less crowded evening, I suggest coming Tuesday or Wednesday."

"I'll keep that in mind in the future. Do you still have us down for tonight?"

The owner looked over his sheet. "Yes, I have you down for eight, Sir Davis. Try to make it there at least fifteen minutes early. It gets a little crazy whenever a scene ends and the crowd starts moving."

Sir glanced around at the sea of people. "Looks like you might want to expand."

"Funny you should say that. We are opening up another club north of here in a few months."

"A wise move. I'd be willing to drive farther to avoid the crowds."

"You'll find everyone is respectful of making room for the scenes. We added extra staff, so there's someone stationed between every adjacent alcove. Even I find this level of activity uncomfortable, although the profits have been staggering. I have you and your sub to thank for that."

Brie blushed, pleased that her film had had a positive impact on the club.

Sir put his hand on the small of Brie's back. "All the credit goes to Miss Bennett, but I'm sure we're both glad to hear The Haven is seeing a positive benefit from the film. Can you tell me if Mistress Luo is scening tonight?"

"As a matter of fact, she's up now at the same alcove you'll be scening at. You should still be able to catch her."

Sir guided Brie through the mass of people, ignoring the number of subs who bowed as he passed. He might not have noticed, but Brie sure did. It only helped to highlight the influence Sir still had in the community, despite having stepped down from his position at the school. It made Brie feel proud—and a little remorseful.

He found a spot where Brie could easily observe the scene, and they were treated to the sight of Boa naked and bound in rope. Brie purred to herself, aroused by the vision of the man kneeling, his arms bound together from the forearms down to his wrists with his palms facing upwards in a sign of surrender. Mistress Luo had bound his arms to his thighs and was finishing it off by wrapping the rope around the back of his neck so that, as she tightened the rope, his head was pulled down into a bowing position.

Because Boa had such a strong, masculine body, Brie found it particularly sensual to see him subdued in rope. His Mistress picked up a candle burning on an elegant metal stand and poured wax over his shoulders and down his back.

He visibly shuddered and let out a low grunt.

"You like that, don't you, Boa?"

"I do, Mistress."

She picked up another candle and proceeded to pour more wax over his back. He groaned even louder.

"This one burns a little hotter."

"It does, Mistress."

"Would you like to try another?"

"Please."

A mischievous smile played on her lips as she poured the third candle's wax onto his shoulders, letting it slowly drip down his back. He let out a low, tortured groan.

"Challenging?" she asked sweetly.

"It is," he answered, his head still bowed.

"One more?"

"Yes, Mistress."

She picked up the fourth candle and held it higher above him. Brie understood that it would help to control the temperature of the wax as it fell. He said nothing when the first drop hit his skin, but as she lowered the candle, he began to shift in his bonds, then let out a deep, masculine moan.

She was certain he must be fully erect, but his impressive shaft was hidden by the placement of his arms. *Such a shame,* she mused. It was crafty of Mistress Luo to tease not only Boa, but the entire audience with her choice of body position. Such a cruelly gifted Domme.

Mistress Luo set down the candle, and knelt beside Boa, whispering something. Brie saw a slight nod from him. Mistress Luo kissed him with her ruby lips, leaving her mark on his cheek, then stood, motioning over one of her other subs. A female sub came up and held her ruby-red cat o' nines out with both hands.

Brie shivered, looking at its wicked knots. *Poor Boa!*

Mistress Luo positioned herself behind him. The first swing from the whip released a cascade of hard wax from his skin. With precision, she lashed his back with enough force that she soon had all of the wax covering the floor.

His Mistress nodded to her waiting sub, who brought rubbing alcohol and a towel. It was then that Brie understood the whipping had only just begun. Boa's Mistress carefully cleaned off his back and dried it before handing the towel back to the female.

Brie watched with trepidation as Mistress Luo positioned herself again, stating, "I am going to count down from five. When the last number leaves your Mistress' lips, your rapture will begin."

Brie's stomach churned when Boa answered, "Thank you, Mistress."

The Asian Domme might have been small in stature, but she was an expert at playing the audience. Everyone watched with bated breath as she cocked back her arm and counted down slowly in her seductive voice.

Brie could barely watch when Mistress Luo finished her countdown and took the first swing. Boa's whole body stiffened upon impact. His Mistress continued to stroke his back hard with the cruel instrument, her rhythm consistent and even.

Instead of focusing on Boa, Brie kept her eyes on Mistress Luo, studying her expression as the Domme released a torrent of lashes. There was a look of deep concentration and affection on her face. This wasn't simply a BDSM scene for all to see, but a chance to witness the deep connection between the Dominant and sub.

It was a powerful exchange; one Brie would not have been able to appreciate before her recent encounter with Rytsar.

By the end of it, Boa was panting with low grunts from the intense character of the instrument.

Mistress Luo stepped back to admire her work before handing the cat o' nines to her attending sub and returning to Boa. The Domme gently ran her hands over Boa's sweaty shoulders and arms, humming softly as she caressed him with her skillful fingers.

"The marks suit your level of submission," she complimented him, loosening the rope around his neck. She lifted his head to kiss him deeply.

"Thank you, Mistress," he replied in a hoarse voice. Brie didn't miss the lowered lids as he looked at his Domme, an indication of a good sub high.

Mistress Luo knelt beside him, and with sensual movements, slowly released Boa from the rope. Her light touches, along with the erotic way she slid the rope over his skin, were arousing to watch. Brie appreciated that the Mistress treated the end of the scene as skillfully as the beginning.

For the sub who was still flying, such treatment accentuated the entire experience. It was the loving actions after a scene that made a submissive feel cared for and cherished.

Sir wrapped his arm around Brie's waist and pressed her against him. It seemed her Master also appreciated

Mistress Luo's work.

One of the staff members walked over to the Mistress and announced their time was up. While the female sub quickly cleaned up the alcove, the tiny Domme helped Boa to his feet and walked him out of the alcove, heading towards the back of the club, presumably for extended aftercare.

Brie glanced at Boa as they passed by, and shuddered when she saw the numerous slashes covering his upper back. No blood had been drawn, but the marks were angry and red, attesting to the onslaught he had endured.

The next couple had already started setting up their scene. Sir leaned down and whispered in Brie's ear, "We're after this."

She nodded, curious what this scene would consist of. She was not familiar with either the Dom or sub, but figured their scene would be a messy one because of the large plastic tarp that had been placed on the floor. The young female placed a chair in the middle of it and stood by as she waited patiently for her next command.

Her Dom was an impressive male with skin like dark chocolate, something Brie found particularly attractive. She watched with fascination as he laid out tiny instruments on a pedestal with his large hands. Although she couldn't see what the objects were, she was excited to find out. It wasn't often she got to observe something new.

Once he was ready, the Master told his slave to undress and straddle the stool, facing the wall so her back was to the audience. She did so, exposing the beautiful complexion of her dark skin. The girl rested her hands against the seat, spreading her legs apart and arching her back so that her round buttocks were displayed beautifully for the crowd. Her pose alone was art.

Brie watched with growing interest as the Dom cleaned off her entire back, from her shoulders all the way down to her shapely ass, swiping it once with a cloth to make sure it was completely dry. It wasn't until he put on surgical gloves that Brie was first alerted to the nature of the scene.

Her heart rate increased when he picked up a long, golden needle.

"Sir, I thought they didn't do blood play here," she said in a worried tone.

Sir looked over at the waiting staff member, who seemed unconcerned. "It appears their policies have changed."

The Dom approached the slave, making sure she saw the needle before he moved to her back. He lightly patted her right ass-cheek with his free hand, letting his slave know the first area of play.

Brie started hyperventilating, visions of Darius holding her down as a child springing to mind.

"What's wrong, Brie?" Sir asked.

"Oh nothing," she said, giggling to hide her apprehension.

When the Master pinched the flesh of his slave and started inserting the long needle into her skin, Brie stopped breathing but failed to notice.

"You're shaking like a leaf," Sir said with concern.

Brie heard blood pounding in her ears just before everything went black and she crumpled to the ground.

Sir picked her up and fought the crowd as he carried her to the back of the club. They met Boa and Mistress Luo, who were on their way out. The Domme smiled at them as they passed, but the smile froze on her lips when she noticed the expression on Brie's face.

Mistress Luo led them to the first open room and quietly shut the door behind them. Sir tried to let her down, but Brie clung to him, whimpering as she pressed her face into his chest—desperate to make the images of Darius go away.

"Shh…shh…it's okay, babygirl."

The pain and humiliation she'd suffered under the bully's hand as a child came rushing back in a tidal wave. Even with Sir holding her tight, she couldn't stop reliving the beatings, the feeling of utter helplessness, and the dread as he'd picked up the needle and started towards her.

"Talk to me."

Brie forced herself to say his name. "Darius…"

"The boy from elementary school," Sir stated rather than questioned.

Brie nodded, not understanding why her emotions were raging out of control after so many years. "I thought I was over it, Sir. Baron helped me get over this."

Sir pressed her against him. "Memories are funny things, babygirl. They can lay dormant for years and then spring up when we least expect it."

The tears started again as she relived Darius repeatedly stabbing her with the used hypodermic needle.

Sir sat her down, understanding that she was locked

in her visions of the past. "Look at me."

She forced herself to look into his eyes, feeling unbearable shame when she did.

Sir surprised her with his raw anger. "I wish I could go back in time and smash the face of that boy before he ever laid a hand on you, but I can't. I can't change the past—nobody can. But you are safe now. No one will hurt you again."

"I know, Sir," she choked.

He cradled her face in his hands. "I want to make sure you're okay. Triggers should never be ignored. They indicate something deeper we must deal with."

She nodded, leaning in to kiss him on the lips, but an image of Darius forcing her lips apart before spitting into her open mouth made her shudder. She refused to break the embrace, concentrating all her attention on Sir's firm lips.

Sir gently scolded her when she broke away. "You failed to be honest with me out there."

Brie slumped in his arms, knowing she had pretended that nothing was wrong—even told him so when he'd specifically asked. "I'm sorry, Sir," she whispered.

"Why did you do that?"

Tears brimmed over as she attempted to explain. "I didn't want past fears to affect the evening we had planned."

"In some ways you're similar to Mary—just as stubborn and foolhardy."

Oh, the humiliation of being compared to Mary. However, Brie could not deny the comparison and shrugged in resignation, smiling sadly at Sir.

"Babygirl, you can't move forward unless you confront the past. Weren't you the one to tell me that not that long ago?"

She sighed, slightly amused her own words were being used against her. "I did say something similar, Sir."

"Lying to me, and yourself, will only lead to trouble."

She looked down at her lap. "I'm sorry I lied, Sir. I know I deserve to be punished for putting you in that position."

Sir lifted her chin. "Tonight you learned something valuable, and I don't believe punishment will add to that knowledge. Let's go home."

"Please, Sir, I still want to scene with you tonight."

"I don't think it would be wise."

"But I need it, Sir. I need to feel your loving dominance over me. It acts like a protective blanket for my soul."

He stared into her eyes, penetrating her with the intensity of his gaze.

"It's *vitally* important to me, Sir."

He nodded, releasing his hold on her. "I understand the reason for your request."

Her lips trembled with gratitude. "I'm so grateful you understand."

He traced his thumb over her bottom lip. "If we do this, you must be completely open with me. No repeating what just happened."

"It won't happen again, Sir. I promise."

"It will be a simple bondage scene, accented with electricity."

"It sounds perfect."

"If you are certain you're ready, then I'll check to see if the last scene is over. You won't be allowed to join me until everything has been cleared."

Brie shivered, hugging herself when Sir left the room. She'd never understood the deep emotional impact a trigger could cause. It had been as if she'd been dragged back in time to a dark place she never wanted to visit again.

It was easy to have more sympathy for Mary now. Yet her own experience left her wondering why Mary was intent on inviting triggers that pushed her into those dark places.

When Sir returned, he graced her with a reassuring smile. "The area is being cleaned as we speak. People were asking about you. Naturally, your friends are concerned."

"Then it's good we're going ahead with the scene, Sir. There's no reason for them to worry about me."

"You're sure about proceeding with this?"

"Absolutely, Master."

"Then prepare to be shocked."

She looked up at him in surprise, then giggled to herself. "That's funny, Sir."

He chuckled as he opened the door. "At least it made you smile."

Sir led her to the middle of the alcove and helped her out of her vinyl corset. Brie looked out into the crowd, feeling her confidence grow as she spied familiar faces.

"Stand on the X and put your arms up, téa."

Brie settled over the large X and put her arms up, looking at the ceiling as the chains were lowered. She appreciated the calming blue hue of the walls and the familiar scent of the ocean breeze floating in the air. Oh, how she loved this particular alcove.

There had been a time in her life when clinking chains would have scared her, but they now brought a welcome thrill. Sir took his time, lavishing her with caresses as he took her wrist and buckled it into the cuff, tightening it until she felt secure. He did the same with the other, leaving trails of ticklish kisses up her arm before buckling it into the cuff. The sensuality of his slow and purposeful movements lured her into his seductive spell.

Sir kissed her on the back of the neck before leaving her side to open the case that held the violet wand. He purposely kept in her line of sight, explaining, "I want you to see what I do. No surprises tonight."

Brie appreciated that he was ensuring she would not feel apprehensive during the scene, safeguarding her success.

She bowed her head in gratitude.

After taking out the violet wand and inserting the rounded glass rod, he plugged it in. Sir nodded to the staff member standing by. The lights were lowered in the alcove, adding to the sensual atmosphere of the scene. When he turned on the wand, the real show began.

Along with the buzzing, came the sparkling purple light. There was excited murmuring in the crowd. Brie figured a few of the new members hadn't seen the electrical toy before, while others knew its delicious feel and were jealous.

She jumped the instant the wand touched her skin,

even though it felt good. There was something about the buzzing and sparks that had all her senses on alert.

"Color, téa? Sir asked, obviously concerned she wasn't as prepared to scene as she'd thought.

"Green, Master," she purred. "The wand has a lot of bark, but not any bite."

With permission given, Sir tickled her with the electricity as he lightly grazed her left side, from her wrist down to her ankle, and then up the right. The light sensation was so enjoyable it was difficult not to squirm in pleasure.

"And now for the chest."

Brie moaned softly when he guided the wand over her breasts, resting momentarily on each nipple, causing them to grow hard as the tool buzzed and crackled with gentle electricity.

"I can tell your body enjoys the stimulation," he murmured in her ear.

She turned her head, hoping to kiss him, but Sir teased her further by coming close enough to her lips that she could feel the warmth of his breath before he pulled away to play with the wand some more.

Brie sighed in pleasurable frustration, loving the way her Master enticed and tortured her.

"I wonder if your pussy is hungry for it too. It's a shame it's covered in vinyl, babygirl. Perhaps some other night..." Sir teased her thighs and stomach with the electric wand, making her wet with desire.

"More, Master," she begged.

"More current?"

"Please."

Sir turned off the wand and switched out the end of the tool, slipping the contact pad into his pants pocket. He slid metal tips onto each finger of his right hand and smiled wickedly at her when he turned the violet wand to a higher setting. "Ready for some real fun?"

She moaned as he approached, knowing Sir was now electrified and that his metal-tipped fingers had the ability to shock her with the current that ran through his body.

"Head back, téa," he ordered. He brushed her hair away and grazed her neck with the metal tips, sending tingles throughout her body. Brie swayed in her chains, moaning loudly in response.

"Color?"

"Violet."

He chuckled. "I take it that's a variant of green."

"Yes, Master," she purred in agreement.

Brie held her breath as he moved his hand, hovering over her right breast. The suspense was excruciating as she waited for him to touch her.

"Watch," he commanded.

She looked down and watched as his fingers cupped her breast. She gasped as the sharp points dragged across her skin as he closed his hand, ending at her erect nipple—which received the stimulation of all five fingers at once.

A ragged moan escaped her lips as the intense current seemed to go straight from her nipple to her groin. Her pussy pulsed in readiness.

Sir moved his hand to her left breast, and smiled as he encircled it with his fingers a quarter-inch from her skin. "What do you want, téa?"

"I want you to touch me, Master," she groaned, her loins aching with need.

"Are you sure?" he teased.

"Please."

"Kiss me."

As she leaned forward to receive his kiss, the metal tips touched her. She moaned into his mouth as he closed his hand, pinching her nipple with his electrified claws.

Those evil hands excited her body, making her jump and squirm as he leisurely explored her skin with the sharp pinpoints of current. The audience loved it, their murmurings of enjoyment competing with the buzz of the violet wand.

"Oh, God, I want you so badly," she whispered when he turned the toy off.

"It's a good thing you have those vinyl panties on, téa, or I would be ramming into you right now."

"Rip them off…" she begged him.

Sir shook his head, but he teased her by getting down on his knees, his lips only inches from her mound. He took a long, appreciative whiff and looked up at her. "I smell your need, babygirl." He kissed her quivering stomach before getting back to his feet and carefully putting his tools in the case.

Brie, along with the crowd, were left hanging with a burning need for release—a release he denied them all.

Blessed Release

I t wasn't until they returned home that Sir made good on his seduction at The Haven. With tender hands and gentle lips, he stoked the burning embers he'd created during their scene together. When he finally pulled off her shorts, they literally dripped with her excitement.

"I think both of us are in need of a shower," Sir told her.

He led Brie into the bathroom and ordered her to stand while he adjusted the temperature of the water. He looked back at her with a charming grin. "I don't want cold water ruining your heat, babygirl."

She twisted where she stood, desperate to put out the flames raging inside her. Her poor pussy ached for him. Being a good submissive, however, she did not complain. She knew the release would be worth the wait.

When Sir was satisfied with the temperature, he stripped down and held out his hand to her. "Shall we?"

Brie moaned with pleasure as the warm water cascaded down her skin, the tiny droplets stimulating her body even more. Sir stepped in behind her and grabbed the bar of soap. Gliding it over her skin, he murmured, "First I lather you, then I bend you over."

Brie moved with him as he covered her body with the luxurious bubbles, the manly scent of his soap an added turn-on. However, what was driving her absolutely wild was his rock-hard cock pressed against her back, announcing his need.

She gasped when the welcome words came as he put the soap down and placed his hand on her back. "Bend over."

With sensual grace, she followed his command, loving the feel of his palm on her back. She braced herself against the tiled wall and looked back at her Master, opening her legs to him.

Sir forced himself inside, bringing tears to Brie's eyes as he filled her aching need with his rock hard shaft.

"I needed that, oh, how I needed that…" she groaned.

"I know," Sir said, grabbing her shoulders to fuck her deeper.

Cupping one hand over her mouth, he increased the tempo of his thrusts, releasing his pent up desire on her body. In a gruff voice he commanded, "Come for me, Brie."

The use of her given name in that passionate moment made her release more powerful and prolonged.

"Oh, damn…" Sir cried, finding himself coming inside her before he wanted. He grabbed her hips and added depth to his final thrusts. Then he lifted her back into a standing position and wrapped his arms around her, his cock wedged inside her still-quivering pussy.

"I wanted to take it slow with you, but there was no denying my lust tonight."

Brie tilted her head back to look at him. "I'm glad you didn't, Sir. I was about to burst into flame."

"The smell of you…"

"I thought for sure you were going to take me right there at The Haven."

He ran his hands over her skin, washing the remaining soap from her body. "I spent too many years fucking trainees in front of a panel. When it comes to taking you…I prefer to be alone."

"I think you stole a year of my life with that little stunt. I feel completely drained, you lust-vampire."

He let his cock slip out of her and turned Brie around, laughing. "Lust-vampire? That's one I've never been called before."

She looked up at him, the hot water still cascading down her back and over her well-spent pussy. "You've earned it, Sir—in spades." She stepped out of the shower, feeling a little faint from the encounter and hot steam.

Sir stayed behind to finish rinsing off. "Go lie down, Brie. I'll join you shortly."

She sprawled out on the bed, feeling utterly and beautifully used. When Sir walked out, he smiled at her. "Did I tucker my little sub out?"

"Completely, Sir."

He crawled into bed and gathered her into his arms. "You never cease to amaze me, Brie. I thought you were mistaken to continue with our plan to scene tonight. Yet here we are, having experienced a very successful evening together."

She caressed his strong jaw, admiring his handsome face. "It's all because of you, Sir. You were so romantic during the scene at The Haven." She propped herself up and looked at him seriously. "I'm grateful that wasn't stolen from me because of what happened."

"It came down to a matter of trust—for both of us."

"Yes." Brie settled back down and thought about the first time they met. "I think I've trusted you from the very beginning, even before I knew who you were."

"Foolish girl," he chided.

"Sir, can I ask you a question?"

"You know my standard answer. You can ask me anything, but that doesn't mean I will answer the question."

"Fair enough. You see, I've been wondering about my entrance video lately."

He raised an eyebrow. "Go on…"

"I think the other trainers must have seen the video I submitted."

"Why do you ask?"

"Well, Lea and I got to talking about it when the trainers in Denver were looking over video submissions during my last visit. It made me wonder about my own video because, up to that point, I'd always assumed you were the only one who saw it."

"The panel always goes through the videos together. It ensures we have a balanced class of submissives." Sir brushed the wet hair from her face. "However, yours was truly a piece of art, Brie. I'd never seen anything as charming as that smile when you threw your socks into the laundry basket."

Brie snuggled up to him, enjoying his flattering critique of her video submission.

"We were all impressed that you did the entire video facing away from the camera with your clothes still on. No entrant had thought to do that before." He glanced at her. "I found it...enchanting."

Brie felt heat rise to her cheeks as she blushed, but she didn't want him to stop. "Was that all you liked about it, Sir?"

Sir chuckled. "No. I also enjoyed the enthusiastic way you sucked the plastic phallus, but it was the look on your face when you penetrated your virginal ass that charmed me the most."

"Charmed you?" Brie felt a twinge of embarrassment thinking back on that moment—her first self-administered anal penetration.

"Based on the form you filled out, it was a shock for all of us to see you perform that act. However, the look of surprise when it slipped in... Ah, well, that was classic. I determined then that I would be the one to introduce your virginal ass to a real cock."

Brie felt pleasurable tingles on hearing his confession. "How did the other trainers react when I called out your name?"

He shook his head. "That little slip almost cost you the spot, babygirl. None of the trainers were pleased, but Gray was especially troubled because he was convinced you must have known me personally."

"But you explained we were strangers, right?"

"I did, but it only seemed to provoke him further. The fact that you were fantasizing about a trainer before you even started the program was a major concern to him." Sir tilted his head and shrugged. "Looking back on it now, I suppose he had a point."

"What did *you* think when I called out your name?"

He grinned. "It was gratifying, Miss Bennett."

"I still can't believe I was brave enough to do the video with that tiny phallus, especially when I..." She blushed profusely, remembering making the entry video for him. "Truly it was only because I was thinking about you that I found the courage to do it. I felt this deep stirring in my soul whenever I thought of you."

"Which brings validity to Gray's initial argument. Luckily, Samantha fought hard for your inclusion into the training program."

Brie looked up in surprise. "What?"

"You heard me correctly." He chuckled, thinking back on it. "Samantha fought to keep you, despite Gray's vehement protests, and was even able to convince Coen that you would be a good fit for our program."

"And they both lived to regret it," she said, laughing to herself.

"No, Brie. Coen respects you, and Samantha...I'm convinced she suffered with issues of jealousy, which clouded her professional judgment. However, she's come to appreciate your abilities and talents."

"Rytsar told me at the cabin that he wanted to talk to you about her."

"And he did, but I do not agree with him."

"What are your thoughts on it, Sir?"

"My friend was damaged by his encounter with Samantha. It's understandable that he still harbors strong feelings against her. It stands to reason that if he can't trust her himself, then he's unable to trust her with anyone he cares about."

"So you aren't concerned about Ms. Clark?"

"Samantha has striven to change her behavior and better herself. She's not the same undisciplined woman she was in college. With that in mind, I have to answer no. I do not worry about her with you, although I completely understand why Durov feels that way. I'm certain I would as well, if it had happened to me."

"Sir, Rytsar asked me a question that has haunted me since."

"What's that?"

"He asked if I trusted her, and I can honestly say that I don't. I trust all of the other trainers, but I don't fully trust Ms. Clark."

Sir nodded sadly, accepting her assessment. "Unfortunately, Samantha has never given you a reason to trust her. Trust must be earned, and she's failed in that regard with you."

"I accepted she was harsh as a trainer, and respected her even when she was harder on me than the others. Knowing how much Lea cares for her, and then learning about your own relationship with her, has helped me to keep a more open mind."

"How did you feel when you met her in Denver?"

"It was *very* different. She seemed easygoing, less abrasive, although just as intense."

"Did you feel differently when you were alone with

her during filming?"

"The truth is I always feel uncertain around her, Sir—even now. I definitely enjoyed filming her scene, but I also felt a bit like a mouse being played with."

"That is an interesting way to put it. Although I know Samantha insists on having the upper hand with subs, I felt the unusual tension between you. As you know, I was forced to call her on it several times, even after your training was over."

"Sir, I never understood her obsession with forcing me to keep my eyes down until this last trip to Russia. After going to Rytsar's club, I can appreciate why eye contact was so important to her. I believe her desire to please him played out in her training of the students."

"You may be right, but Durov doesn't particularly care about eye contact when it comes to his own submissives. He demanded it from Samantha because she was a Dominant, and it pleased him knowing it ate her up inside to obey."

"Always the sadist."

Sir frowned. "I still can't reconcile what happened between them...but I would never willingly put you in harm's way. Rytsar may be blinded by what happened between them, but I'm not. I can see both sides and have seen the devastation it caused. However, if you do not feel safe around Samantha, I will make sure you are not left alone with her again. I trust your instincts, babygirl. I always have."

"If I ever feel unsafe, Sir, I promise to let you know."

Sir mused aloud, "I suppose in the end it comes

down to whether you believe people can change. I do, up to a point. Put in the same situation with the same stimuli, most will revert back to the way they were. It's the reason I encouraged Samantha to give up on Durov. There was no hope and never could be, given their history. Since then, she has matured and found her place within the BDSM community." He looked at Brie and asked her solemnly, "Do you believe people can change?"

"Of course, Sir. I'm not the person I was before I met you."

He gave her a sly smile. "I've never admitted this to anyone, but I kept your submission entry. I couldn't delete such a masterpiece."

Brie laughed, shocked but pleased by his admission. "I can't believe you kept my video, Sir."

"I was reckless when it came to you—right from the start. Tell me, babygirl, would you like to revisit that moment in your life?"

"Please, Sir."

Brie snuggled up to him when he settled back on the bed with his laptop. She smiled to herself when she saw he had named the file 'MasterpieceAKABrie'. As soon as he hit play, she could tell just how nervous she'd been by the way she'd smiled at the camera and then looked away shyly.

Brie buried her head in his shoulder, embarrassed to watch. But when she heard her own laughter, she looked back at the screen and saw herself licking the tiny phallus.

"It was so incredibly small, Sir."

"It was meant not to intimidate the entrants."

It was hard not to burn with mortification when she started making mewing sounds as she attempted to deep-throat the thin tool. However, Brie's juices started flowing at the sound of her own moans as she watched herself lay down on the bed and masturbate with it.

"I enjoyed hearing your unique noises. It made the experience that much more intimate and personal."

Brie cuddled closer to him, very much enjoying his take on her video.

There was a pause in the action when she went to buy the lubricant from the corner store. When the camera flipped back on, Brie saw herself pulling off her socks. She distinctly remembered throwing them into the hamper and yelling, "Score!" when she made the basket.

Sir stopped the video when she looked back at the camera and smiled. "This is the exact moment you stole my heart. That open smile in the middle of a sexual scene." He shook his head, his eyes warm with affection. "It was perfect."

He hit play, and Brie had to suffer the embarrassment of watching herself coat the tiny phallus with far too much lubricant and then tell herself out loud to relax as she tried to push it inside her anus without success.

"I thought you were done here—we all did—but then you…"

Brie blushed as she watched herself get on all fours, now facing the camera. She knew what was coming and buried her head in his shoulder again.

"Watch," he commanded gently.

Brie looked back at the computer just as the toy

slipped inside, and she heard herself gasp.

Sir stopped the video again. "That tiny gasp and the surprised look on your face sealed my fate."

Brie covered her eyes, humiliated by the humorous expression captured on the screen. Sir pulled her hand away and forced her to look at herself. "It was your reaction right after this that convinced us all you had real potential. You closed your eyes, deciding if you wanted to continue." Sir smiled tenderly at her. "Despite your fears and inexperience, you chose to go on. You weren't playing for the camera. You weren't forcing yourself to do something you didn't want to do. No, you were being true to your nature and we all recognized that strength in you."

"I remember it like it was yesterday, Sir. I was scared to introduce a foreign object into my body, but all I had to do was imagine that it was you. I wanted to know what it felt like to have you deep inside that forbidden place."

Sir placed his hand on her upper thigh. "That desire came across loud and clear in your video."

She giggled. "To think I have Ms. Clark to thank for my acceptance into the program..." Remembering back to those beginning sessions, Brie stated, "I do remember that she was complimentary in her critiques the first couple of days, before she grew to hate me."

"It wasn't until my claiming of you that I noticed her claws come out. She felt very protective of me, although there was no reason for it."

"How did she find out when it was done in private?"

"The Center has cameras in every room, Brie. I fully

expected the trainers would see it. However, I'm a man who knows what he wants and refuses to play the coward by hiding his actions. I wanted you, so I claimed you before anyone else could fuck that fine ass of yours." Sir lightly caressed her buttocks with his hands before grabbing them possessively.

"That was all I wanted, Sir. In fact, I was upset when the class ended that second night and I thought you weren't going to keep your promise to me."

"Ah, but I wasn't about to ruin our intimate moment by inviting a live audience." He pressed her body against his. "No, I wanted our first time to be as private as possible."

"Even at the cost of losing your position at the Center...which eventually *did* happen, Sir." Brie let out a heavy sigh. "I hate that you had to give up your job to collar me."

"Some things are worth the sacrifice." Sir kissed her on the lips as he slipped his fingers between her legs...

His cell phone rang, and Sir's hand instantly froze. "That is Thompson's ringtone," he explained as he disengaged to reach for the phone.

Brie watched his expression carefully as Sir talked to his lawyer. Although his voice remained calm, she noticed his lips twitch several times during the conversation.

"Interesting... I suggest you set up a meeting at your office if that's the case." He paused for a moment, then replied, "Fine, I'll pay for the flight. Thursday will work for me. We'll speak then."

Sir stared at Brie after he hung up, looking a bit

stunned. "The test results came back positive. It appears I have a half-sister."

Brie wasn't sure how she felt about the news, but forced herself to reply optimistically. "That's amazing, Sir."

He shook his head, a smile playing on his lips. "To think I have a sibling I never knew about…"

"I take it you're meeting her this week, based on the part of the conversation I heard."

Sir took Brie's hands in his. "*We're* meeting her this week."

"How strange it will be to meet her in person. Oh, my gosh, I wonder if she looks like you."

Sir surprised her by growling under his breath, "I hope for her sake Lilly looks nothing like her father. I don't think I could handle it, given the part he played in my father's death. In fact, the idea of meeting her brings back memories I'd rather not deal with."

"But we'll face them together, Sir," Brie vowed, putting her hands on his chest. "This is a positive step forward for you."

He shook his head slowly as he gazed at the lock of her brown hair he was rolling between his fingers. "Although I'm curious about this girl, there are still so many questions that have yet to be answered."

Lilly

Meeting Lilly at Thompson's law office reminded Brie of the last meeting Sir had had with his mother. She sincerely hoped it would be the *only* similarity.

"I don't care if it seems odd or cold to her," Sir stated as they rode up on the elevator. "I still have my reservations, and a professional environment will help to remove emotion from the equation if this goes poorly."

"I understand your caution, Sir, given what you've been through."

Sir hesitated with his hand on the doorknob to the meeting room. "Why do I have the unsettling feeling this is going to change my life in ways I can't imagine?"

Brie put her hand on his. "Because it will. You have family again."

Together, they opened the door and walked inside. Sir immediately stopped and stood silent as he glared at Lilly.

The girl stood up to greet him, a pleasant smile on her face—an eerily familiar smile.

"I can't believe it!" she cried, running up to Sir with her arms open wide. To Brie's horror, the girl was a perfect replica of Sir's mother.

Sir kept his arm outstretched, keeping his distance as he shook the woman's hand in a stiff manner. "There can be no doubt that you are my mother's daughter."

Lilly looked up at him, smiling. "And you! No doubt you are the son of a handsome Italian."

Sir dropped her hand abruptly and turned to shut the door.

Brie understood the emotional jolt he'd suffered, and spoke up to relieve some of the tension in the room. "Hi, I'm Brie Bennett. It's nice to meet you, Lilly."

The girl took Brie's hand, but then enfolded her in a hug. "Yes, I've read all about you. I haven't seen your film yet, but I certainly plan to someday soon."

Brie was taken aback when Lilly kissed her on the cheek, but she didn't have time to react, because Lilly was back on Sir, grabbing his hand and pulling him towards the table. "There's so much to talk about!"

Lilly sat down and covered her face with her hands, exclaiming excitedly, "Oh, my God, you're really my brother. This is so weird…"

Sir was slower to sit down, and pulled out the seat beside him so Brie could join him. "I admit this is a shock for me as well."

"Why in the world would Momma keep you a secret?"

Sir looked at her solemnly. "I assume you are aware of our past."

"Well, naturally I've looked you up on the internet,

but still... I don't get why she would want to keep you and me apart like that."

He answered without any emotion, "I'm a part of her past she wanted to forget."

Lilly shook her head, smiling at Sir. "But I don't get it. She loved being a mother. I can't imagine her abandoning you like that."

"The two of us did not end on good terms."

Without asking, Lilly grabbed his hand and squeezed it. "You know, I read about the tragic death of your father. Both Mom and you must have been devastated. I've heard unexpected deaths can break families apart."

"He didn't die tragically; he killed himself because of her," Sir stated, pulling his hand away.

But Lilly would have none of it, and grabbed it back. "I can't believe Momma could be so cruel as to leave you behind, Thane. It was wrong for her to do that."

Sir looked down at her hand gripping his but, to Brie's surprise, he didn't pull away. "I do not know the person you claim her to be. My experience with Ruth has shown her to be a heartless human being, and she proved that to me time and again."

"Thane...I hope you don't mind if I call you that," Lilly said with an infectious grin.

"I'm not opposed to it."

"Thane, I can't explain my mother's actions, but I sincerely hope you and I can become friends and break down the walls she built. Neither of us should be alone in this world."

Sir glanced at Brie. "I'm not alone."

Lilly smiled, quickly correcting herself. "No, that's

not what I meant, but surely you'll agree it's wrong to be deprived of family."

"You should talk to your mother about that, but unfortunately she can't face your justified wrath."

Lilly patted his hand before withdrawing hers. "I don't hate her; I just want to understand her reasons for doing this to us. Momma was only loving and kind to me. Whatever she did to you, that was not how she treated me." She smiled at Sir apologetically. "But we should leave that for another day. Really, all I want to do is get to know you better."

"Agreed."

Lilly raised her eyebrows playfully. "So I read that you run your own consulting company and that you used to be headmaster of a school. That's all fine and good, but what do you do for fun?"

Sir looked at her oddly and did not reply.

"I mean, what are your hobbies? What do you do in your spare time?"

"Spare time? What the hell is that?" Sir laughed.

Brie wrapped her arm around his and smiled at Lilly. "The two of us are always on the run. If we aren't working, we're…doing things together." She laid her head on Sir's shoulder.

"I get that you two are a couple, but seriously, Thane. What do you enjoy doing on your own? Surely a man as independent as you are has other interests."

Brie felt a twinge of resentment. It felt as if the question was meant to be a jab against her, not asked out of simple curiosity.

"Although we haven't had the time recently, I do

enjoy the opera."

Lilly's eyes lit up. "I do too! Have you seen Carmen? It's my favorite one."

Sir shook his head. "No, I have not. Its storyline reminds me too much of my mother. I could only wish she had ended like that."

Tears formed in Lilly's eyes. "How could you say that? I…"

Sir sighed before reaching over and taking her hand. "I'm sorry. I think both of us must tread lightly when talking about her."

Lilly dabbed her eyes with a tissue and nodded. "Still, I really think you should see it. I love that opera."

"I will keep it in mind, Lilly," Sir said kindly.

"So other than our mutual love of opera, what else do we have in common?"

When Sir failed to answer, Brie chimed in. "He's a talented cook."

Sir shook his head. "Talented is a stretch. Let's just say that I enjoy my time in the kitchen."

Lilly grinned. "I grew up in the kitchen with Momma. She was always experimenting with new dishes."

Sir seemed interested in that fact and asked, "What did she cook?"

"Oh, every French dish under the sun. Momma always said the more butter and cream, the better."

"No Italian then?"

"No, Momma said she hated Itali—" Lilly's face fell and she immediately apologized. "Oh God, I'm sorry."

Sir shook it off. "That's fine. I think we're done here."

"Done? But we've barely started. I'll be more careful with my words, Thane. I *need* to get to know you better. Please don't brush me off."

He could not be swayed by her pleas, and informed her, "This is enough for now. We've established communication."

Lilly got up from the table and rushed over, wrapping her arms around him. "I want so much more than that. Please, Thane."

It was surreal to see a younger version of his mother hugging Sir so tightly. Brie hoped it brought him comfort, because it made her skin crawl.

"I'm staying at the Rayburn hotel for the next couple of days. I would love to get together again. Please say yes."

Sir broke away from her and stood up, holding out his hand to Brie. "Miss Bennett and I have a busy week ahead, but I'll consider it."

"Thanks again for the plane ticket and hotel," Lilly blurted. "I can't tell you how much this means to me."

"Don't give it another thought."

"Well, I'm sure you heard from your lawyer that I'm a junior accountant in New York and can barely make ends meet even with a roommate." She laughed. "So getting the chance to come to LA is a dream come true for me, but meeting my long-lost big brother totally blows my mind!"

"It is equally unsettling for me."

Lilly shook her head, giving him a humorous look. "No, Thane, it's not unsettling. It's wonderful!"

He chuckled lightly. "Fine, it's wonderful."

The next morning, an envelope arrived for Sir via courier. Inside was a note and a smaller, golden envelope. Sir read it out loud to Brie:

Dear Thane,

Just talking about Carmen got me excited. Imagine my surprise when I found out it's playing here! It took some doing, but I obtained tickets. Please think of it as a thank you for the travel, and a chance for you and I to get to know each other in a less formal environment.

Love,
Lilly, your little sis

Sir opened the second envelope and pulled out a single ticket. He looked at her apologetically.

Brie smiled as she put her arm around his waist. "It's for the best, Sir. You should spend time alone together."

"Unfortunately, it's on the same night as Mr. Gallant's party. I had hoped to speak to Miss Wilson there to see how she's faring. Even though I trust Captain with her care, as her former trainer, I feel responsible and wanted to check in."

"I'll talk with her, Sir. I suspect she'll be more open with me anyway."

"Keep it civil this time."

Brie blushed, remembering her last phone call with Mary. "I won't attack her, no matter how rude she is."

Sir's voice took on a softer tone when he asked, "What are your impressions of Lilly, Brie?"

She collected her thoughts before answering, not wanting to put a negative spin on something so personal to Sir. "To be fair, I've only met her once."

"And…"

"I'm unsure."

"As am I. I'm trying not to be suspicious of Lilly's intentions, but her look is uncanny and quite disturbing to me."

"I know what you mean," Brie confessed, grateful he'd been the one to bring it up. "But it's unfair to judge a person by their appearance. Although I understand that, it's hard not to think of your mother whenever I look at her."

"I was surprised by her financial situation."

"You mean that she's living modestly like any normal person her age? I was surprised by that too, Sir. I naturally assumed your mother would have raised a spoiled brat, but maybe she honestly wanted to give Lilly a fair chance in the world."

"Or maybe Lilly recently lost all her money and has always known about me," Sir speculated.

Brie hated to even go there. The last thing Sir needed was another Ruth in his life. "Did Mr. Thompson find out anything on her that contradicts her story?"

"No, everything checks out, but…"

Brie was relieved to hear it. "You just need time, Sir. Time to get to know Lilly so you can see her for the person she really is. That's all." She kissed him on the lips. "You're a good judge of character. Trust your instincts."

Sir shook his head, growling angrily. "When it comes to my mother and anything associated with her, I find myself assuming only one thing."

Brie took the ticket from his hand. "Maybe, just this once, you should let down your guard and get to know your sister."

"Sister…what an odd concept."

"But your new reality."

Mary Quite Un-Contrary

S ir left for the opera an hour before Brie was to leave for the party at Mr. Gallant's. Just before he headed out the door, Sir handed her a red box. "Open it."

Brie lifted the lid and took out the delicate red mask that was nestled in tissue paper. "It's beautiful, Sir, but what's this for?"

"The Gallants are requiring masks for the evening."

"Really?" She looked it over, suddenly intrigued.

"Yes, his wife thought masks would add to the festivities tonight."

"Oh, Sir. Now I'm really unhappy you won't be joining me."

"I had this shipped from Italy," he told her, taking the mask and placing it over her eyes. He tied it into place and turned her back around to admire her. "You look stunning, babygirl."

It was important that he spend time with his sister, Brie knew that, but the chance to see Sir wearing a mask would have been such a rare treat. It was hard not to pout.

Sir kissed her on the lips. "Rest assured, we'll have our own private mask party."

Brie purred. "Good, because I want to make love to you in a mask."

He pinched her butt. "Aren't you the kinky one?"

She giggled, but the merriment ceased the moment he shut the door on his way out. Going to this gathering without him would be a depressing ordeal, no matter what the reason for it.

Standing on Mr. Gallant's doorstep a short time later, Brie sighed self-consciously. It wasn't easy being there alone wearing her mask. It just felt odd without Sir.

All that changed when Ena answered the door wearing a breathtaking mask of gold. "Miss Bennett, don't you look lovely? Thank you for coming tonight. Please, won't you come in?"

Brie was greeted by the sound of laughter echoing from deeper within the house.

"We've been waiting for you," Ena explained. "You're the last of our guests."

Brie had come fifteen minutes early and was surprised to hear it, but automatically apologized. "Oh, I'm sorry."

"Don't be. You came exactly on time."

Mr. Gallant's wife escorted her into the main room, where Brie was overjoyed to see some of her favorite people. Not only were Captain, Candy and Mary there, but also Marquis, Celestia, Master Coen, as well as his three female subs. Rounding out the group was a tall, copper-toned man Brie instantly recognized as Nosh, the head of the Dominant Training Center.

Mr. Gallant walked up to Brie wearing a silver mask, which made him look even more distinguished and refined in her eyes. "Welcome, Miss Bennett."

"It's wonderful to see you again, Mr. Gallant! Is it okay if I hug you?" Brie asked, fighting the urge to throw her arms around him.

"As I only acted as your teacher, I see no breach in protocol."

Brie grinned as she hugged her tiny but formidable teacher. To her delight, Mr. Gallant's two girls came bouncing into the room. "Must we leave, Daddy?" the oldest protested sweetly. "Everyone looks so beautiful."

"This is an evening for adults, girls," he gently reminded them.

The youngest pushed out her bottom lip. "Please, Daddy?"

Mr. Gallant tweaked her nose. "If I hear no more complaints, we'll treat you and your friends to a masked gala of your own."

The girls squealed and showered him with kisses. Ena came up and told them, "Now girls, your ride is here. Promise me you won't keep the Hendersons up giggling until all hours of the night."

"We won't, Mommy," the two answered in unison. The youngest turned to Brie and said, "I like your mask best," before skipping out the door.

"Hurry along," Mr. Gallant said, picking up their

overnight bags. "We don't want to keep your friends waiting."

Ena turned to Brie and tsked good-naturedly. "My girls have their father wrapped around their little fingers."

"It's quite charming," Brie confessed. "It's nice to see serious Doms can still be doting fathers."

"And devoted husbands," Ena added, smiling as she shut the door once Mr. Gallant had walked back in.

Her former teacher explained to Brie, "Although we can relax a bit, we keep things relatively vanilla even when the girls are gone. Should one of our children walk through the door unexpectedly or neighbors happen to look through the window, we don't want them to be shocked by what they see."

Brie smiled, respecting his wish to protect his family. "Understood, Mr. Gallant."

She spied Mary kneeling in the corner and excused herself to find out what Blonde Nemesis was up to. As she approached, she couldn't help admiring Mary's sparkly emerald mask.

"Nice eye wear, woman," she complimented, then whispered, "Are you being punished?"

"No, bitch. Vader said I struggle with not being the center of attention. Now go away," she hissed without looking up. "You're going to ruin it for me."

"Whatever…"

Brie scooted in the direction of Candy and Celestia, who were waving her over enthusiastically. Candy wore a sapphire mask that matched Mary's emerald one, while the art that graced Celestia's face was of midnight black, accented with pinpoints of crystal around the eyes. It reminded Brie of a night sky, which was poetic, since that was the name Marquis had given her.

Brie asked Candy in a confidential tone, "Is Mary being punished?"

Candy smiled, glancing over at her. "No, what you see there is a woman who wants to impress."

"Impress Captain?" Brie asked, unable to hide her surprise.

"She's grown close to my Master, and takes what he says to heart," Candy explained. "Mary has made significant strides since joining our household." She added with a laugh, "It almost makes up for everything she put us through the first few days."

"Oh, my," Celestia exclaimed.

Brie snorted. "I can only imagine."

Candy looked over at Mary with pride. "Surprisingly, she has a deep philosophical side to her, and a gentleness few see."

"Gentle? Mary?!" Brie scoffed. "That is *not* a word I would ever use to describe her."

Candy smiled in Captain's direction. "My Master sees right through walls. You'd be surprised what he discovers when he tears them down."

"Well, I for one never imagined Mary would try so hard," Brie said, giving Candy a grateful squeeze. "Thank you for letting her invade your home. My friend really needed you."

"It's been our pleasure, Brie. You helped me, and we've been able to help someone else. That's how it's supposed to work, right?"

"Yes, but let's face it, I had it a lot easier than you." Brie turned to Celestia, not wanting her to feel left out of the conversation. "So tell me, how has life been treating you lately?"

"I've been doing well, and would love to tell you all about it over a cup of coffee sometime."

"We should all get together more often," Candy suggested.

"Sounds great, but I can't make any plans until after the wedding. Once the raw footage is shot and the wedding is behind me, *then* I'll have a more open calendar."

Candy nudged her playfully. "Sure you will..."

Brie grinned. "It's been freaking crazy lately, but thankfully it'll all be over in a few months."

"Yes, it will, Miss Bennett," Marquis said, strolling up to join them. His mask was like Celestia's, but all black, perfectly framing the dangerous glint in his eyes. "If you have any reservations about the upcoming nuptials, now would be the time to state them."

She felt heat rush to her cheeks. "No, Marquis Gray. The wedding, I'm looking forward to. It's everything *before* the wedding that's getting to me."

"Like Sir Davis's dying mother?"

Brie gasped. Leave it to Marquis to hit the tenderest mark without warning or mercy.

"We're working through it, Marquis Gray."

"And his sister?" he pressed.

"He's coming to know her."

"I'm curious, Miss Bennett. What were your first impressions of the girl?"

Brie knew she needed to step carefully with Marquis, or she would invite a cascade of difficult questions she didn't want to address. "It's really too soon to make judgments."

Marquis raised his eyebrow. "I asked for your first impression."

"To be fair, I find that she looks too similar to Sir's mother for me to judge."

"So if you *were* to make a judgment, it would not be favorable at this point?"

Brie shook her head. "No, that's not what I meant…"

Master Nosh walked up to the group. The chiseled, masculine mask he wore hinted at his Native American heritage, but it was the long, painted black tears on the mask that drew Brie's attention. She was startled to find he was staring intently at her from under the mask.

Mr. Gallant moved in to formally introduce them. "I don't believe you've been properly introduced, Miss Bennett. This is Master Nosh, Head of Dominant Training. Master Nosh, this is Brie Bennett, former student of our school and resident film director."

Brie bowed. "It is an honor, Master Nosh."

She remembered the Master from her training days, when she and the other submissives had been given the unique opportunity to critique training Doms at the Center. That had been the same day Faelan had impressed her with the power of a simple feather.

The intimidating Dom only nodded to Brie, saying nothing.

"Master Nosh is a man of few words," Master Coen

announced, joining them with his arms draped around two of his submissives. His smile was barely visible underneath the metal mask that covered three-quarters of his face. It gave him a distinctive gladiator vibe.

His girls each wore the same style of mask, made of colorful cock-feathers which contrasted nicely with the cold metal of his mask.

"I was told you never had a chance to discuss your film with Nosh, Miss Bennett, but he is a wealth of knowledge."

Brie appreciated Master Coen's lead-in, and took the opportunity to address the Master personally. "I hope you will consider sharing some of that knowledge with me, Master Nosh. I know many fans of the original documentary hoped for a peek at the Dominant Training Center."

After an extended pause, the man spoke in a voice so deep it made Brie's insides tremble. "I will consider it."

He turned to Master Coen and put his hand on his shoulder, silently gesturing to the rest of the group.

"Yes, I suppose now is as good a time as any," Master Coen conceded, speaking to the entire room. "Master Nosh and the Gallants already know the news I'm about to share."

Mr. Gallant kissed Ena lightly on the back of her hand and nodded to Master Coen in encouragement.

He stunned the room with his next pronouncement. "I am stepping down as Headmaster."

Silence settled over the room.

"Don't look so glum. I've been recruited to head the first sister school in Australia."

"Oh, now that *is* interesting…" Marquis Gray remarked.

Mr. Gallant gave Master Coen a congratulatory pat on the back. "Reason enough for celebration tonight."

Ena disappeared into the kitchen, returning with a small but decadent-looking chocolate cake. "Who would like a piece?"

It seemed to break the dazed spell Master Coen had caused, and Captain requested a large slice. He proceeded to sit down on the couch, placing the plate on the coffee table. "Pet, *lief*, come."

Brie watched Mary stand up and walk over to him, gracefully kneeling on one side of Captain while Candy knelt on the other. He waited until the entire party had been served before he cut a small piece for Candy and then another bite for Mary. Darned if Blonde Nemesis didn't demurely eat from the fork Captain offered with a slight blush on her cheeks.

Mr. Gallant told everyone, "Although this is a vanilla affair, try to have a little fun tonight."

Master Coen wanted nothing to do with the cake, but for personal entertainment he insisted his submissives share a piece without using utensils. He watched with obvious pleasure as they seductively licked the frosting off each other's fingers.

Mr. Gallant watched with amusement and swiped his finger over the top of Ena's cake, spreading the rich chocolate over her lip. "Charming," he praised. "You look good enough to eat." He leaned over and removed the offending chocolate with a sensuous lick. "Delicious…"

Brie smiled to herself, nibbling at her cake.

"Oh, Brie, do you remember when you brought over the custard?" Celestia asked, giggling.

Brie whimpered, "Must we bring that up?"

Celestia leaned in and whispered, "You'll never know how much that endeared you to Marquis. He enjoys seeing his students humbled. He believes everyone needs a little grounding now and then." She nodded discreetly at Mary, who was looking up at Captain with adoration as she accepted another bite. "Whenever one of their students overcomes an obstacle, it is a victory for the entire staff."

Brie smiled. "I agree with that sentiment. Seeing Mary dig herself out from her violent past is truly inspiring."

Celestia mused aloud, "You can't help but wonder what Faelan would have thought..."

Mr. Gallant cleared his throat, making both Brie and Celestia jump. Brie was sure she was about to be reprimanded for gossiping when he took her to the side to speak to her alone.

"Captain and I believe you and Mary should talk."

"I would love to, Mr. Gallant."

"Please use our bedroom upstairs for privacy's sake. It's the last door down the hall."

Brie walked over to Mary to ask her to join her upstairs, and was pleasantly startled when Mary deferred to Captain. "May I leave the room, Vader?"

He placed his hand on her head. "Yes, *lief*. Enjoy your time with your friend."

"Thank you, Vader." Brie was stunned that Mary

seemed genuinely content under Captain's rule. She turned to Brie and smiled. "Lead on, Stinky Cheese."

"Mr. Gallant said we could use his bedroom upstairs," Brie informed her as they walked out of the room.

"His bedroom? Now that sounds naughty, doesn't it?" Mary murmured, placing her hand on the railing as she headed up the stairs.

"You're not going to do anything weird, are you?"

Mary tossed her hair back and shrugged. "We're just going to talk. Right?"

Mr. Gallant's bedroom had impressive double doors that opened into a large room complete with an oversized bed, a reading nook and a wet bar. Mary looked around, running her hands over the oak counters of the bar and the red leather of a chair next to a bookcase. "Talk about a *Master* suite."

"We're not here to snoop in Mr. Gallant's room," Brie warned. "We're supposed to be talking."

"You're such a wet blanket, Brie" she pouted, flopping onto the king-sized bed and looking up at Brie. "So talk."

"I'm not saying a word until you sit on the edge of the bed. Show Mr. Gallant and Ena a little respect, damn it."

Mary spread her hands over the comforter as if she were making a snow angel. "Just think, Brie. Our illustrious teacher fucks his submissive on this very bed."

Although it was an alluring thought, Brie didn't want to start down that path with Mary. "That's it," she snapped. "We're sitting on the floor—a place you're used to."

Mary rolled her eyes, but flopped onto the floor, crossing her legs. She kept looking around the room, fascinated by it. "I bet we're the first students ever to see this hallowed place. Why do you think he has a bar in his bedroom? Don't you think that's a bit strange?"

"I don't care, Mary. Talk to me about you. How have things been going with Captain?"

Mary let out a long sigh. "Getting all serious on me, huh? You're no fun."

"Well?"

She looked away when she answered. "It's fine. No, actually it's better than fine."

"So what's been going on since we last talked? Did he stop making you watch them kiss and snuggle?"

"No," Mary said with a slight grin. "I'm...getting used to that."

Brie nudged her shoulder. "I knew it! You're an old softie inside. I couldn't believe that you let him feed you in front of us tonight. It looked like you actually enjoyed the attention."

"Shut the fuck up."

"Deny it all you want, but it was obvious to everyone in the room and I found it sweet."

"Now I know you're just trying to piss me off."

"No." Brie put her arm around Mary. "I'm not. There's a real change in you. Why can't you just admit it?"

Mary paused, suddenly getting serious on Brie. "I don't want to jinx it."

"Jinx what?"

"At first, being around them was nauseating. But the more I saw how Captain was with Candy, how he genuinely cared for her, the more…"

"The more you wanted it for yourself?"

Mary snarled, "I'm not lusting over Candy's man, if that's what you're implying."

"No, you twit. I meant you want to be treated that way by another man."

Mary rolled her eyes again. "You totally don't get it."

Brie growled in frustration. "Then explain it to me."

"I…" Mary seemed to struggle with the words. "I feel accepted for the first time in my life… I've never felt that way before, and I don't want to lose it."

"Accepted you how? Because Todd accepted you, fangs and all. What's different?"

"They accept me for me, damn it," she said, pointing to herself. "Just me. Not for my looks or how great I can give a blow job…and I'm far better than you—just saying."

Brie ignored the jab, realizing the importance of what Mary was sharing. "So they accept you as a person, not as a sex object?"

"No, you idiot! What I'm trying to tell you is that they accept me as…" She could hardly say the word, and just whispered, "….family."

Brie felt a chill go through her and goosebumps rose on her skin. It took everything not to cry, but she knew how much Mary hated tears and valiantly fought them off. "That's profound, Mary."

"I know. A few times at their home, when we were just hanging out there, not doing anything special, I felt whole." Mary's lips trembled. "I've never felt that before, Brie. Ever."

"You deserve to feel that way, my friend."

She shook her head. "I was afraid Captain might be a mental-case making me call him Vader. I was sure he was planning to act out some Daddy fantasy on me, but fuck it, he really means it. He's been respectful to me this entire time—no wandering touches, no flirtations or sexual glances. You know what I mean. Those stolen glances that let you know where their mind's really at."

"Sure."

"In the past I would have been offended that he was ignoring me. Hell, that's how I relate to all men. But staying with Captain has been different. I really feel a connection to him that has nothing to do with sex."

"Like a father figure."

"Exactly."

"What about Candy?"

Mary smiled. "My relationship with Candy is just the icing on the cake. I see every woman as competition, but she's the first one who doesn't bring out my cutthroat nature, and it's not because she isn't hot. It's just that...I don't feel the need to compete with her."

"Wow, that's huge."

"See, I thought of all the people I know, you might understand. It is huge—it's *fucking* huge! Even my shrink is impressed."

"So I take it that your counseling is going well?"

"Reiny, that's my pet name for him—God, he hates it—he tells me I've been much more open this time around. Seems hitting rock-bottom has that effect on the strong."

"Did he say that or did you?"

"Well, maybe not in those exact words, but let's just say he's impressed with my progress."

"That's great, Mary. Really great. Sir will be thrilled to hear it."

"Yeah," she growled. "Don't think I'm unaware that everyone's been talking about me behind my back."

"Seriously, you're not *that* important. People are concerned, yes, but Miss Wilson isn't the main topic of conversation."

"Sure I'm not…"

Brie let out a snort. "I can't tell if you're fucking with me or being serious."

Mary grinned, her eyes sparkling mischievously.

"Well, at least it's good to see you acting like yourself again."

"Brie, I have to ask…"

"What? Anything."

She paused for a long time. "How's Faelan? I haven't stopped thinking about him, not for a second since he left."

Brie frowned, wishing she had something positive to share with her. "I'm really sorry, Mary. I have no idea where he is and I haven't heard from him since we left the commune."

"Don't you think it's fucked up? I'm finally getting my shit together, but he'll never know I love him?" A tear escaped, but Mary brushed it away angrily.

"He knew that, Mary," Brie assured her, trying to stop her voice from quavering. "I believe that's why he never gave up on you."

Mary buried her face in her hands, trying unsuccessfully to hold back tears.

Brie looked away, knowing she was about to fall apart herself. She was angry that fate had been so cruel to them.

Mary took a couple of deep breaths, brushing away her tears. "Well, I'm done talking."

They stood up together, but Mary walked over to the dresser mirror to fix her face and fluff her hair before presenting herself to the group again. She turned and smiled wickedly at Brie. "Since this is the only time I'll ever be in here…"

Before Brie could stop her, Mary went behind the bar and tried to open the cupboards. "They're all locked! I bet this bar is really just a cover to hide all his toys from the kids." She slapped her hands on the counter in frustration. "Damn, I was hoping to see what kind of kink he's into."

"OMG, Mary, get away from there! You have no decorum whatsoever."

Mary held her arms up in surrender. "Fine, but don't tell me you weren't curious." She shut the double doors to the bedroom, murmuring, "Some other time, Gallant…"

Brie would never admit it to Mary, but she *was* curious. Mr. Gallant was a compelling mystery that she'd often contemplated, and it appeared the man was destined to remain that way.

Darkness

Brie arrived to an empty home, even though she didn't get in until after two in the morning. She wasn't surprised, however, knowing Sir and Lilly had a lifetime to catch up on.

She drifted into the bedroom and was getting ready for bed when she noticed Sir's journal open on his nightstand. She inadvertently glanced at it, wondering if it might hold a fantasy of his. When she saw the word 'Mother', she immediately picked it up to read, wanting to know what he was feeling.

Mother

You are darkness

You seek to destroy

Betrayal as your heritage

Cruelty your legacy

And yet

I care

Forever damned

By the love that ruined me
Yet haunts me...
Still

Brie sat down, rubbing her hands over the words, wishing she could remove the profound pain expressed on the page. She knew Sir still struggled with memories from the past, and meeting his sister had only helped to stir the nightmares he'd kept buried deep within.

She closed his journal and kissed it, placing it back on the nightstand. "May tonight bring you a new level of peace, Sir."

Not being the least bit sleepy, Brie decided to wander back out to the couch with a large blanket to cuddle in. She turned on the TV for background noise and whipped out her laptop to work on her film while she waited for Sir's return.

She was in the middle of reviewing the footage between Rytsar and his young sub when she could have sworn she heard his name on the TV. She glanced up and turned up the volume when a picture of him flashed across the screen.

"...Rachel, I have a little tidbit about the man we've been hearing so much about."

"Do tell!"

"I did a little digging and discovered our Russian hero is the very same Rytsar Durov from that naughty underground hit last summer."

"Get out!"

The two women giggled as they fanned themselves.

"Of course, it's tragic what happened to the girl, but how dreamy it must have been to be rescued by him."

"Those big buff arms…"

Brie quickly googled Rytsar's name and was shocked to find a recent news article detailing the captive girl's ordeal. Upon further investigation, she found that the culprit of the leak was the girl herself. Apparently she had fallen for the Russian Dom and wanted the whole world to know of his heroism.

Brie started hyperventilating, afraid this young woman's zeal might end up costing Rytsar his freedom or even his life. She picked up the phone and called his private cell, a feeling of unease setting in when he didn't pick up quickly enough.

"Hello?" he finally answered in his thick Russian accent.

"Rytsar, have you heard what's happened? Stephanie, that young girl you saved, just told the world who you are and what you did."

He cursed under his breath. "Titov specifically told her and her family to remain silent. Why would she do this?"

"I'm not sure, but I think it might be a case of hero-worship. This girl's going on and on about how you saved her from the bad guys. Luckily, the only substantial information I've been able to glean from the internet is your name and your main residence in Moscow. Get ready, though—the phone is about to start ringing off the hook."

Rytsar snorted. "No, the landline was destroyed in the fire, *radost moya*. They will not be able to reach me, and only those I trust have this number."

"What if you get in trouble because of this?"

"The girl knows little," he assured her. "Titov spoke to her extensively before they left the Motherland. Besides, without a body or witnesses, there is no crime. Do not fret—you will not be tied in any way to the event."

"That's right, you don't know! They've already associated you with my documentary."

Rytsar sounded amused rather than upset. "You Americans and your fascination with the men of Mother Russia."

"This isn't a laughing matter!"

He lowered his voice, speaking calmly to her. "I do not foresee it being an issue for you—I will ensure it."

"What about you?"

"Huh! If something were to befall me, I would not alter the course of my actions. I am at peace, *radost moya*. There is no reason to be concerned."

Brie's lip trembled when she confessed, "I couldn't handle it if anything were to happen to you."

"It won't."

Not willing to end their phone call and still longing to know about his past, Brie prodded hesitantly, "Rytsar?"

"*Da?*"

"Can I ask you what happened to Tatyana?"

The phone went silent.

"Rytsar?"

He whispered softly to himself, "Tatyana..." It seemed as if simply hearing her name had flooded him with images and memories. "Yes, *radost moya*, I will tell you of her."

Brie turned off the TV and wrapped the blanket around her, chilled by the haunted tone of his voice.

"I wouldn't have known her if it weren't for Titov. We were boyhood comrades, he and I, making trouble in the streets of Moscow. The two of us got into many scrapes together." He chuckled to himself. "You wouldn't believe the numerous whippings I suffered under my father's belt because of our mischief—all worth it."

Brie giggled, imagining the little hellion Rytsar must have been.

"But as often as I hung around Titov, I never really noticed his little sister until she turned sixteen. I'd been invited over for dinner one evening, and she greeted me at the door. It was then that I was confronted by those dangerously arched eyebrows and blossoming curves." He grunted with pleasure at the memory. "It was as if a light bulb had suddenly been switched on and I was consumed by only one thought: *MINE!*"

Brie smiled to herself, imagining that moment.

"However, Tatyana told everyone she was saving herself for the right man. She purposely ignored me, inviting the chase. But I was content to bide my time, in no particular hurry to settle down just yet."

He growled under his breath. "It wasn't long after that Titov started running with a different crowd—people I refused to associate with. I warned him, but he was young and foolish, full of ambition. He and I went our separate ways, but I never forgot about Tatyana. I knew she was waiting for me to claim her."

"On her eighteenth birthday he came banging on my door, shouting that Tatyana had gone missing. We looked everywhere for her only to discover that one of his new 'comrades' had amassed a huge gambling debt. The boy had needed to turn a quick profit or lose his life as payment. Rather than face his fate, the maggot kidnapped Tatyana and sold her to a foreign buyer. The two of us beat the shit out of him to get the information, only to miss rescuing her by mere minutes—*minutes*!"

A tear ran down Brie's cheek at the thought of the young woman being kidnapped and raped repeatedly, believing she'd been forsaken, never knowing how close she'd come to being saved…

"We were forced to spend the next five months playing a perverse game of cat and mouse as we tracked her from owner to owner." Rytsar's tone became more subdued when he told Brie, "She was broken, just skin and bones, huddled in a corner, high on heroin the day we finally caught up with her. When Titov approached Tatyana, she offered herself to him, begging her brother to be gentle. We foolishly thought we'd saved her when we brought her back home, but what did we know?"

"But you did save her," Brie insisted.

"*Nyet.* We failed to understand how shattered she was. Her family and I bought her smiles and assurances, and took heart when she forced herself to start eating again. The reality was that she was appeasing us, just biding her time—whether she knew it or not."

Brie felt chills when she heard his next words. "I'll never forget the day she killed herself. I'm not a man for sentimentalities, but I bought her yellow flowers. It was a national holiday and I was in a rare mood to celebrate." He paused, his voice becoming bitter. "Now I only associate yellow with blood… I hate flowers."

"Why did she do it when she had so much to live for?"

"Tatyana told me once that she was tainted beyond repair, and it made me furious. I swore to her that anyone who dared tell her that would answer to me personally. I failed to listen, *radost moya*. She was not talking about other people's perceptions of her, but her own."

Brie heard the heartbreak in his voice when Rytsar confessed, "You cannot fix the broken, no matter how much you want to. She was the *one*—my mate and the future mother of my children. When that maggot took her, he not only stole her future, but mine and that of generations to come."

Rytsar pounded his chest, howling in rage, the sound of sickening thuds carrying over the phone line. Tears rolled down Brie's cheeks as she listened, knowing there was nothing she could do to ease his suffering or the unbearable loss he felt.

When the terrifying sounds stopped, an eerie silence followed.

"Rytsar?" she cried out softly.

His hoarse voice cut through the darkness like a beacon of hope. "That's why this girl is important. Titov and I need her. We need her not only to survive—but to *live*."

Those words haunted Brie after they hung up. She

put her computer away, no longer able to work. Instead she folded the blanket, laying it on the arm of the couch before heading off to bed. Just as she flicked off the lights, she heard the ding of the elevator in the hallway.

She didn't know what possessed her, but she jumped into bed and pretended to be asleep.

Sir lingered out in the hallway for an unusually long period of time. Finally his welcome footsteps started towards the bedroom and she buried her head in the pillow. She heard him step inside the threshold, but then stop.

After several long, agonizing moments, Brie snuck a peek to see what was going on. Sir was standing in front of her, looking down with a knowing smile on his lips.

"Just wake up?"

She looked up at him guiltily. "No, never fell asleep."

He chuckled as he started loosening his tie. "I noticed the blanket was still warm in the other room, and you don't usually sleep with your face smashed into the pillow."

She pulled back the covers and invited him to bed. "How was the opera with your sister, Sir?"

The sparkle in his eye said it all. "It went far better than I'd hoped. Tell me, how was the party?"

"It was wonderful, Sir."

"Since neither of us feels like sleeping, why don't we fill each other in on the night's events? Waiting until morning only ensures we'll forget a detail or two."

"Did you hear about Rytsar and the girl?"

Sir nodded. "Durov texted me. I'll be watching the situation closely, but for now all we can do is wait, trusting it will blow over without incident."

"Rytsar told me about Tatyana."

"Such an unfortunate loss," Sir stated, a sad look in his eyes. "Although it spurred him to come to the States as an exchange student, it's sobering to think that his loss became my gain. I wouldn't be where I am today if I hadn't met Durov in those early college years."

"Life is a strange journey."

Sir grunted his agreement.

Brie wanted to lighten the mood, so she fluffed up the pillows and propped herself against the headboard, snuggling against Sir when he joined her in bed. "Why don't you tell me all about Lilly?"

To her delight, he shared everything. Not only what they'd discussed, but his thoughts and impressions throughout the evening. Any concerns Brie had had about being left out disappeared as Sir detailed the entire night. What struck her most was how excited he seemed. Sir radiated energy, as if he were riding on an emotional high.

"Until tonight, I can't say I would have understood when you shared Miss Wilson's assertion that one could feel whole again. But it seems, for a brief moment, I experienced that this evening."

Although Brie found that admission surprising, she was completely unprepared for Sir's next revelation.

"Brie, in the spirit of feeling whole..." He pulled her closer. "I have a serious question for you."

"Of course, Sir. You can ask me anything."

He cupped her chin and smiled. "For this conversation, call me Thane."

Brie's interest was piqued, and she leaned in to kiss him. "My pleasure…Thane." She loved the way his given name rolled off her tongue when she said it—so sexy and romantic.

"There's something that my grandfather did on his wedding night. He spoke of it as if it was the greatest experience of his life. One not to be missed."

"Oh! You have my mind spinning now. I can't even imagine what you're about to say."

Sir gently stroked her cheek, causing tiny, tingling jolts of electricity to run over her skin. "My grandfather said the most beautiful moment of his life was when he made love to my grandmother on their wedding night. He said it was knowing they *might* conceive a child from the union that made it so singular."

Sir continued, tracing her lips with his fingertip. "My father hinted at the same thing. It's tradition for our family—no contraception allowed on the honeymoon. Simply a man and his woman, committing their lives in the most intimate way."

He gently pressed her head to his chest, stroking Brie's hair as he looked down at her. "You've mentioned you want children, Brie."

She nodded, but added softly, "When you're ready."

"Durov was not wrong to point out I'm not getting any younger. I feel, if this is truly the direction you want to go, we should start a family sooner rather than later. There's no sense in putting it off."

Brie lifted her head. "While I can appreciate what you're saying, S—Thane, I have my documentary to think of, and you're still building your overseas business."

"True enough, which is why you must be absolutely certain this is the path you want to take. I'm willing to have children, but only if we begin now."

The reality of what he was suggesting was both thrilling and frightening to her. "*Now?*"

"If we conceive quickly, which is no guarantee, I will still be in my mid-forties by the time the oldest is barely ten. It's now or never, Brie."

She bit her lip, adrenaline flowing through her veins as she seriously considered his proposal. "A family when I'm still just a kid myself?"

"My grandmother was nineteen when she had her first child, and my mother…only twenty-two."

Brie took a deep breath as reality began to sink in. "I would have to put my career on hold."

"Probably, at least for a few years once you get pregnant. If we do this, I want you to take care of yourself and the baby. No late nights, and no last-minute deadlines."

She shook her head in disbelief. "I have to admit, when you started the conversation tonight, this was so *not* the direction I thought it was headed."

"Durov made a nuisance of himself in Russia, but it made me think. He was right to push the issue. If you wish to be a mother, we need to begin soon."

Brie stroked his jaw, rough with morning stubble. "Do you really want to have a baby with me, Thane Davis?"

The tenderness in Sir's eyes melted her heart. "Yes, Brie. I want you to have my child." He smiled as he wiped away a tear that had formed in her eye. "But there's something you have to do for me."

"What's that?"

"You need to stop taking your birth control pills, and we won't be having intercourse again until our wedding night."

Her jaw dropped. "For two whole months?"

Sir nodded, grinning when he saw her look of shock. "When we make love again, Miss Bennett, it will be as man and wife."

"I can't even imagine…"

"Now, that's not to say we won't enjoy each other's company. It just won't be in the traditional manner."

"Oh, thank goodness! I think I'd shrivel up and die otherwise," she said laughing. Then Brie looked at Sir seriously. "In case this is our last chance for a while, I'd like to make love with you tonight."

Sir kissed her on the lips, slipping his tongue into her mouth. "Let's…"

Brie scooted out from under him. "Did you buy a mask for tonight's party?"

He nodded towards the nightstand. Brie opened the drawer and pulled out a black mask lined in silver. "I like this very much, it's so stylish. Do you mind if I put it on you?"

He lifted his head and she slipped it over his eyes. She sat back to take in the sight of Sir lying naked in the bed, wearing nothing but the sexy mask. "You are one handsome man, Mr. Davis."

He smiled and held up his hands. "Have your way, Miss Bennett."

Brie growled lustfully at the invitation and climbed onto him, straddling his already hardening cock. She grabbed his wrists and forced them over his head. "Resistance is futile."

She put pressure on his wrists, using them for leverage as she slowly slid her wet pussy over his shaft. "I want you to feel how much I love you." She kissed him on the lips and left a trail of kisses down his chest. "I cherish every part of you."

Sir groaned when she flicked her tongue over his nipple. She moved to the other and nibbled lightly before flicking her tongue again. "Do you want me, Thane?"

"What do you think?" he replied, thrusting his pelvis upwards so she could feel the hardness of his shaft.

Brie smiled as she lifted up to slowly descend on his cock. She threw her head back and moaned as she took the fullness of it. "You feel so good inside me." Taking her time, Brie rolled her hips, purposely moving slowly so he would feel every movement, every slight tilt of her pelvis.

Sir stared up at her, totally infatuated with her dangling breasts. They proved too much of a temptation, and he reached up to play with them.

"God, you're beautiful," he murmured. Brie purred, loving the feel of his hands on her nipples, caressing and tugging on them. Sir leaned up and took a mouthful, grazing her nipple with his tongue before sucking it.

"I crave your mouth," she moaned, pressing herself against him.

He amped up the suction as he showered equal attention on each breast. Brie rewarded his attention with deeper penetration and faster pelvic thrusts, which drove both of them to the edge.

Brie suddenly stopped and laid her head on his chest, listening to his wildly beating heart. She smiled up at him once it had slowed back down to a normal rhythm. "I treasure that heart."

She sat up again, wiggling her pussy against his base as she caressed his body with her fingers, from his muscular thighs and toned stomach to his hairy chest and talented hands.

"Every inch of you is sensual and pleasing," she confessed.

"Show me how much I please you."

Brie bit her lip, bracing her hands against his chest as she began rolling her hips again. "I will not stop this time," she warned him. "I'm going to use your gorgeous body for my own pleasure." She took him at just the right angle to rub the ridge of his shaft against her G-Spot. With quick, short strokes, she built up the delicious tension until chills coursed through her.

"I'm close," she whispered, throwing her head back and concentrating on his cock rubbing against that sweet, swollen area deep inside her. Her breath became shallow as her body tensed for release.

"Let me make it easy for you," Sir growled huskily. He reached around, teasing her clit with his fingers. She moaned in pure bliss, creeping ever closer to the edge. When she was on the precipice, he slowly slipped his finger inside her ass.

Brie cried out in ecstasy as her body began its rhythmic dance around his cock. "Come with me, Thane."

He pulled her down on top of him, wrapping his arms around her as he thrust his pulsing shaft into her, filling her with his seed.

Brie lay there panting afterwards, smiling. "I love when you come inside me."

He gave a contented sigh. "I do too, babygirl."

They lay in each other's arms as the sun peeked over the horizon, bathing their bedroom with its light.

"Welcome to a new day, Sir."

He leaned forward and kissed the top of her head. "Brie."

She immediately looked up, responding to the serious tone of his voice.

"I want you to carefully weigh what we've discussed. This decision will change the course of our lives—not only our careers, but our relationship as well."

The gravity of the decision was not lost on her. She curled up under the comforter as Sir got up to pull down the shades. The complexity of their situation was overwhelming. She was about to change what they had—the perfect life she knew and loved—to grasp for something out of reach.

It was risky.

But when she closed her eyes, she saw herself holding Thane's child and she knew peace...

The Mission

A few days later Sir sat Brie down, explaining that he had an important mission for her. "Lilly would like us to fly to China to visit our mother together. However, I need you to return to Denver."

She felt a twinge of jealousy that Lilly was trying to leave her out. "My documentary can wait, Sir."

"It's not about the film, Brie. Mr. Wallace needs at least one of us to be with him right now."

The mention of Faelan completely stunned her and she gasped, fearing the worst. "Is he dying?"

"Yes…and no." Sir took her hand in his. "He will die without intervention, but a donor has been located and Wallace has finally been given a date for surgery."

"A donor for what, Sir?"

"He lost a kidney in that car accident years ago. Unfortunately, his remaining kidney was also damaged in the crash and has begun to fail."

"So he's getting a kidney replacement?"

"Yes, but because of his blood type that has proved a difficult issue."

"Couldn't his parents just donate one of theirs?" she asked naively.

"No. He has the particular honor of being O negative, which means he is a universal donor but can only receive organs from another O negative patient. They are extremely rare."

"But you said a donor *has* been found?"

Sir nodded. "Yes. In the most unlikely of places. After Mr. Wallace apprised me of his situation while we were at the Sanctuary, I began contacting people who might be able to help within our community back in LA. When no donor was found, I expanded the search. Naturally, donors are less likely to give up a healthy kidney to a complete stranger. The surgery itself requires months of recovery, extreme pain, and the very real loss of a functioning kidney."

"That must be why Todd gave up all hope."

"The likelihood of finding a donor in time was next to impossible, but fate has been generous and a man overseas has agreed to donate his organ. The surgery will take place next week, but I want you to be there for Mr. Wallace now. I've been told he's not doing well, physically or mentally. For this procedure to succeed, he must be as healthy as possible going in to the operating room."

"Of course I want to help, Sir, but my preference is to be there for *you*."

He kissed her tenderly on the lips. "I cherish your support which is why I plan to fly with you to Denver, before I continue on to New York to pick up Lilly."

Brie could not hide her disappointment at being left behind. "I wanted to be there when you saw your mother again."

"I wish that were possible, babygirl. Sometimes life pulls us in different directions and we have to do what's best for all concerned."

"Will you two be deciding whether to let her die?"

"I hope to convince Lilly that it's time. However, she refuses to even discuss it until she sees our mother in person. I can't blame her; it's not easy to end a life."

"But if you decide to pull the plug, you *will* send for me."

"Brie, you are a part of me. I will need you there when the time comes."

She laid her head against his shoulder and sighed. "I hate that there is so much going on at once, and none of this is easy."

"Life isn't easy, I learned that a long time ago. We must each find our happiness during the hardships if we are to survive." Sir took her hand and kissed it. "*You* are my happiness."

"And you are mine, Sir."

"Before we start this unwanted separation, I have a pleasant task for you to complete. I've arranged for your mother to come this weekend. Do you think you can find a wedding dress in two days, my dear?"

Brie squealed, overjoyed at the prospect of visiting with her mother and finding *the* dress. "I will leave no stone unturned."

"I have only two requirements for the gown."

She raised an eyebrow, curious what they might be. "Please share."

"I want it to be pearl-white and have a low, swooping back." He rubbed the small of her back sensually with his fingertips. "I hope to see a hint of your brand."

She blushed, pleased by his requests.

"Money is no object. However, I do have an added challenge for you and your mother—to add to the thrill of the hunt. I'm giving you ten thousand."

Brie's jaw dropped. "Ten thousand dollars?"

"Yes, but what you don't spend can go to the charity of your mother's choice."

"I love the nature of this challenge, Sir," she said, giddy with excitement.

"Good, but don't feel any shame if you end up giving five dollars to your mother's charity. I want you to purchase the dress of your dreams. One that makes you feel elegant inside and out."

Brie threw herself at Sir. "Man, I can't wait to marry you!"

He chuckled. "On a more serious note, have you given any more thought to having children?"

Brie nodded, answering his question by marching into the bathroom and bringing back her two packets of pills. She knelt at Sir's feet and held them up to him. "I stopped taking them last night."

He took the two cases from her and deftly tossed them. They made a satisfying clunk when they landed in the wastepaper basket. Sir took her hands and kissed each upturned palm. "You and I are officially starting a family, babygirl."

Brie's mother came late that Friday night and the two began mapping out the dress shops they wanted to visit. "Let's go for the big wedding shops in outlying cities first—they should have the best selection of discount racks—and then we can concentrate on the smaller boutiques if we need to."

Sir interjected, "I don't want you to find a bargain deal, Brie. Your dress should be as exquisite as you are."

Her mother cooed. "Oh, I love that you talk to my daughter that way." She placed her hand on his shoulder. "But you must trust me that I will not fail in this duty I've been given."

Brie grinned at Sir. "Getting my mom on the case was a wise decision. She has a nose for quality bargains."

"As long as you're happy with the dress," Sir replied.

"Don't worry, Thane. She will be, but you shouldn't expect to see us until late tonight. There's no rest for the wicked."

He smiled charmingly at her mother. "I hardly consider a mother and daughter shopping for wedding dresses as being wicked."

"Oh, you don't know me at all, son," her mother quipped. "This woman is going *whole* milk in her latte today."

Sir laughed. "I'll be sure to warn the cops."

As they were leaving, her mother confided, "I like your man, sweetie. A sense of humor goes a long way in a marriage."

"He and his friends are all kinds of funny, Mom."

She shook her head. "I can only imagine. Actually..." She giggled. "I'm afraid to."

They spent the day running from shop to shop, trying on many beautiful gowns, but not one stirred Brie's soul. She came back that night feeling defeated, until she smelled the enticing aroma of Sir's *ribollita* floating from their apartment.

"What?! He cooks too?" her mother asked in astonishment as they walked through the door.

"Thane's a true Renaissance man, Mom. Maybe now you can understand why I love him so much."

Sir had set the table simply and let them dish up their own bowls, but he insisted on finishing their dishes. Brie's mom was taken by surprise when he sprinkled her bowl with aged parmesan and a swirl of olive oil.

"Oh! I've never had anyone put oil on my stew before," she said, giggling.

"Trust me, it makes the dish," Brie assured her. The dinner was accented with many sounds of pleasure as her mother enjoyed the fruits of Sir's labor.

He wore a pleased smile as he watched the two women consume the meal he'd made. "So no dress today, Brie?" he asked, once he'd finished his bowl.

She put down her spoon and shrugged. "I'm sorry."

"Do I need to repeat that getting a bargain is not the goal? I don't want my challenge to stop you from buying the dress you want."

"It wasn't that. It's just...I never found one that felt right. There was one this afternoon that was close, but something was missing. I didn't love it."

Brie's mother patted her hand. "Don't worry about it, Brianna. Tomorrow we'll try the smaller shops. I'm positive the dress you're looking for is out there. We will find it, *and* at a price that will make you sing."

Brie smiled, accepting her mother's promise. In typical 'mom' fashion, she insisted on doing the dishes when Brie stood up and started to clean off the table.

Sir protested and tried to stop her. "You're a guest in our home."

"Nonsense. We're practically family, and family helps out. Besides, you cooked the meal. It's the least I can do."

He nodded graciously, consenting to her offer and retiring to the adjoining room. Brie smiled every time she glanced at Sir while hand-drying his cooking tools.

"I wish your father could see this," her mother stated wistfully.

"He will someday, at a holiday gathering, when he's bouncing his grandson on his knee."

Her mother stopped scrubbing the pot to look at Brie. "Are you planning on having children?" she asked in a hushed whisper.

Brie smiled shyly and nodded.

Her mother's eyes suddenly filled with tears. "I never dared hope…"

Brie wrapped her arms around her mom and they both started crying. It wasn't until then that she fully understood the dreams her parents had given up in their desire to be supportive of her marriage.

"Is everything okay in there?" Sir asked from the couch.

They smiled as they wiped away each other's tears. "Everything is perfect, Thane," Brie answered. She looked at her mother and they started laughing.

"Good. I prefer laughter to tears."

Her mother elbowed Brie. "A keeper for sure."

The next morning, the two women started out early, driving over an hour and a half to get to a little shop south of LA. It was in an older area, and the shop was so tiny that Brie wasn't sure she even wanted to stop, but her mother insisted.

When they entered the establishment they were greeted by an elderly couple. "Welcome, ladies! Which one of you is getting married?" the old gentleman asked.

Brie's mother giggled. "Aren't you so cute?" She pushed Brie forward. "My daughter is looking for a dress, but she has specific requirements, so why don't we cut to the chase and not waste any time?"

The grandmotherly woman took both of Brie's hands. "What are you looking for, dear heart?"

Brie blushed, moved by the woman's gentle eyes. "My future husband requested a pearl-white dress with an exposed back."

The woman's eyes lit up. "Do you like lace?"

"I do," Brie answered enthusiastically.

She turned to her husband. "It finally happened."

"What?" Brie's mother asked, laughing nervously at their odd behavior.

"Go get the gown," she said to him in a reverent tone.

The old man smiled and disappeared into the back of the shop. While he was retrieving the dress, the shopkeeper explained, "Years ago, a young woman ordered a beautiful wedding gown but she never returned to claim it."

He came back out with the dress and smiled as he lifted it for Brie to see. The woman continued, "The front is covered in Italian lace, but the silk sheath underneath will flatter your figure because of its princess neckline. So modest and elegant."

She led Brie into the changing room to help her into the gown.

"Momma," Brie called once it was on, grazing the delicate lace with her fingertips.

Italian lace…

When her mother entered the fitting room, she stopped short and put her hand to her lips, tears welling up in her eyes.

Brie slowly turned to behold the splendor of the back as the shopkeeper shared, "The back has a simple but beautiful scoop line, and just look at that train… We took a hard hit when the young woman never showed up, but I always trusted the right bride would come along."

Brie smiled at she looked at the dress in the mirror. It accentuated her back, still in keeping with the elegance of the front, and the gown showed off her curves with tasteful sensuality. The best part—the one she knew Sir would appreciate most—was that it showed the slightest hint of her brand.

"Of course, it will need to be fitted, but oh…" the old woman sighed, holding her hands over her heart, "this dress was made for you."

The woman called out to her husband, "Honey, you *have* to see this!" She hit his arm excitedly when he pushed back the curtain. "Didn't I tell you it would find a home?"

He smiled looking at the dress and then up at Brie before turning to his wife. "Yes, you did, dear. I should never have doubted you."

Brie played with the pearl buttons that ran up the length of her arm, loving that little touch. "So now I must ask the dreaded question. How much?"

The woman smiled hesitantly, clasping her hands together in a nervous manner. "Twenty-five hundred."

It was far cheaper than Brie had expected. She looked at her mother and smiled, an inspiration coming to her. "Do you have a veil to go with this?"

"Oh, I have the perfect one. It will complement the dress but won't detract."

While the couple hunted for the veil, Brie whispered in her mother's ear. To her delight, her mom nodded in enthusiastic agreement.

The couple returned a short time later with a simple handmade veil. The old woman placed it on Brie's head with a loving touch as she smoothed out the fine lace. "There!"

Brie turned and looked at the mirror. She was overcome with a prickling sensation she knew well. It suddenly felt real, all of it—the wedding, a life with Thane, growing old together.

Without any hesitation, Brie told the shopkeepers, "I would like to pay twenty-five hundred for the veil."

"No!" the old man scoffed.

"Consider it a finder's fee. You've had this dress waiting for me for years. I won't take no for an answer. You've made me unbelievably happy today," Brie gushed.

Her mother chimed in, "That's true for both of us, and I'm sure a certain groom will be thanking you later."

The woman blushed, waving away the praise, but then she asked timidly, "Would you mind sending us a picture of the wedding? It would mean so much to us."

Brie's mother grabbed a business card from the counter. "Consider it done."

On the drive home, Brie took a detour to the area above the city where Sir had taken her on several occasions. Even though it held difficult memories, it was a stunning view of the city she'd grown to love, and she wanted to share it with her mother.

Brie pulled to the side of the road and they got out to take in the expansive city below.

"So you really like it here?" her mother asked.

"I love it, Mom. I couldn't be happier."

"I can appreciate that better now. For us, everything was overshadowed by our own shock. But now...now I've seen you two together in your home, with no strained conversations, no guards up, I can see how truly happy you are."

"It's kind of hard to do that around Dad."

"You know he means well, and it'll make him happy to know how well this trip went. Brianna, he only wants what's best, and you can't blame us for being uncomfortable with this whole...BDSM thing. I mean, who wants to know what their children do in the bedroom?"

Brie blushed. "Although I can appreciate that, our lifestyle choice is so much more, Mom. There's a community of people we can count on, and lifelong friendships that have changed me for the better. Most people my age walk around in a daze, coming home from work to waste time on their phones, watching TV or playing on their computers." She stated proudly, "But I don't waste my time, Mom. I'm constantly challenging myself to grow as a person with Sir's—I mean Thane's—help."

Her mother wrapped her arm around Brie. "You can call him Sir around me, sweetie. Your father finds it disturbing, but it doesn't bother me in the least."

Brie smiled as she pointed in the direction of the tobacco shop down below. "I was sitting in a dead end job, just trying to make ends meet while filming shorts on the weekend. I would still be there if it hadn't been for Sir."

"No, honey. I believe you would eventually have found your way into the industry."

Brie shrugged. "I guess we'll never know, but what I *do* know is that I love the path I'm on, and I wouldn't change a thing. How many people can say that?"

Her mother looked over the city as she squeezed her daughter. "Not many, Brianna. Not many."

Although it was hard to see her mother head back to Nebraska, it was even harder watching Sir pack for his trip to China.

"I don't want you to go, Sir," she lamented as he folded a shirt and laid it in his suitcase.

"You need to start packing too, babygirl."

"I know, but I've been putting it off because I don't want us to be separated again."

Sir stopped what he was doing and walked over to her. "Mr. Wallace is struggling. He needs your encouragement, and I must go to China."

"I understand…" Brie sighed. "We can't change what is happening, but I hate these separations."

"It's amusing you feel that way, since you're a film director by trade. You did *know* it requires a lot of travel."

"Yeah, yeah…"

"In that vein, I suggest you use any free time in Denver to film missing elements while you have people at your disposal. Time is running out."

"I know, because soon we'll be getting married!" she squealed with joy.

"Yes, we will, Miss Bennett." He grabbed a fistful of hair and pulled her head back, kissing her deeply. "So let's get through this difficult part, focusing on the fact that the best is yet to come."

When Brie lay in his arms that night, she could barely keep her eyes open.

"Go to sleep, babygirl," Sir whispered.

She dutifully closed her eyes and images of her bridal dress came to mind. Brie could just imagine walking down the aisle, seeing Sir's expression when he beheld her in the gown for the first time…

Tono's smile took her breath away. "Are you ready, toriko?"

She smoothed out the exquisite dress, admiring the lace details of the ivory gown before looking up at him and answering confident-

ly, "Yes, Tono."

The Asian Dom held out a piece of jute and she purred, willingly offering her wrist to him.

Tono gently wrapped the rope around her delicate wrist, creating a decorative pattern of rosettes.

Brie examined it closely when he was done, sighing in contentment. "It's beautiful." She looked up at him, tears in her eyes. "It's perfect, just like you."

He took her hand and gently kissed the rope. "No tears, toriko."

She wiped them away, giggling. Brie pushed her shoulders back and lifted her chin as the music began to play. She clutched the bouquet of orchids and smiled. Her moment was at hand...

Brie started when she woke.

"What were you dreaming about?" Sir asked, stroking her cheek. "I was watching you and saw a hint of a smile on those sweet lips."

"I was dreaming about my wedding." Brie blushed, confused about why she'd been dreaming about Tono. Thankfully Sir could not see the flush on her cheeks.

"Good," he said in a low, soothing voice. Sir tucked her against him. "Now try to go back to sleep. We both have a long day ahead."

Brie nodded, but she lay there wide awake, pondering her dream. Why was she dreaming about Tono, and what the heck did it mean?

Departure

Brie boarded the plane headed to Denver, along with a bunch of groggy passengers. It was four in the morning and, other than the businessmen, the majority of travelers were slow-moving and sleepy. She waited patiently for people to stuff their luggage into the upper bins, but had to quell her irritation when some of them took far too long to do that simple task.

At one point, an older woman tried several times to lift her baggage above her head to slide it into the bin. When the man in front of Brie refused to extend his help, she pressed past him to offer her assistance.

"Thank you, dear."

"My pleasure, ma'am."

"It's so rare to find gracious young folk these days."

"They're still around, ma'am. They're just harder to find at four o'clock in the morning."

The woman laughed, insisting that Brie stay as she dug in her purse and produced a piece of wrapped candy. "It's from my secret stash. Best chocolate in the world," she stated proudly, handing it to Brie.

Brie thanked the woman before moving farther down the aisle, curious where Sir could be hiding. She was surprised to spot her handsome Master at the very back of the plane.

"Fancy finding you here," she said when she reached him.

Sir winked as he took her bag and placed it in the bin above. He took out a blanket and a small pillow, handing them both to her.

"Oh no, Sir. There's no way I'm going back to sleep."

He leaned in and said in a seductive whisper, "Trust me, téa, you're going to need it."

Her heart quickened at the use of her sub name in public. "Ah…well then, thank you." She scooted to the window seat and buckled herself in, placing the two items on her lap. "I've never ridden at the back of a plane with you before, Mr. Davis," she teased flirtatiously.

"When I noticed this wasn't going to be a full flight, I decided we should take advantage of the fact," he replied, grazing his finger under her chin.

"I must say I like your way of thinking," she replied, adding in the barest of whispers, "…Master."

He sat down and commanded in a low voice, "Lay your head on the pillow and cover up with the blanket."

Brie grinned to herself as she followed his directions, propping the small pillow against the window, wondering what he had planned for her.

After the plane had taken off and the lights had been turned off so the passengers could sleep, Sir instructed her to close her eyes. She was thrilled by the mystery behind his unusual requests, and lowered her eyelids, refusing to open them even when the *ding* above her announced that the seatbelt sign had been turned off.

Brie heard Sir take out his computer, followed by a light clicking sound as he started to type.

It was pure torture sitting there with her eyes closed, not knowing what he was up to, but she remained still, as per his command. When a stewardess passed by, Brie heard Sir stop her and explain, "We would prefer not to be disturbed for the rest of the flight, but I would appreciate a glass of water."

"Certainly, sir."

Brie giggled to herself, never tiring of hearing service people unwittingly call him by his title.

After the woman returned with his water, she heard him pull down her tray and placed the plastic cup on it before lifting the armrest between them. "Now, téa, unbuckle yourself. Place the pillow on my shoulder and lay your head against it while you cover my lap with an extra portion of your blanket."

They released their belts at the same time and Brie nonchalantly switched her position, settling her head on Sir's shoulder. She noticed a movie playing on his computer screen and noted that he was wearing ear-phones to make it appear as if he were actively watching the show.

Brie dutifully closed her eyes again, waiting for her next set of instructions.

After several minutes, Sir murmured, "Slowly, so no one will notice, slide your hand under my boxers and take hold of my cock."

Her pussy contracted pleasantly upon hearing his command. With measured movements, she headed towards that sacred spot between her Master's legs. Sir had already unfastened his slacks, allowing Brie easy access to his shaft. Her fingers slipped under the elastic band of the boxers and grasped his rigid shaft.

"Don't move."

She remained still as she felt his hand move ever so slowly under her skirt and beneath her lace panties. He rested his hand over her mound and stopped.

They stayed like that—neither moving—but each deliciously aware of the other's hand resting on their sex.

Finally, Sir directed her, "Slight movements. Don't attract attention."

Brie pressed herself closer against him to get a better reach and gently squeezed and released his cock in her hand. Sir met the challenge by separating her outer lips and lightly fingering her clit. She was already moist due to the nature of her task, and he whispered appreciatively, "Nice and wet."

Brie remained silent, keeping up the ruse of a sleeping partner as she explored his shaft with imperceptible movements. She was rewarded with drops of pre-come on the head of his shaft, announcing his enjoyment to her without words. She used the coveted liquid as lubricant, rubbing it over his shaft as she stroked him ever so slowly, his manhood throbbing in response.

Not to be outdone, Sir increased the tempo of his fingering, causing her to unconsciously arch her back.

"Stay still," he warned.

Brie nestled her head against his shoulder, squeezing his shaft tighter as she stroked him, longing to make the challenge as difficult for him as it was for her. She heard the stewardess pass by again and froze. When Sir assured her that the woman hadn't given them a second glance, she started up again.

Brie relished the fact that this was their first 'official' encounter since deciding to have a child. He had warned her there would be no intercourse until their wedding night, but he'd also promised they would enjoy alternative activities while they waited. Never in a million years would she have guessed they'd be pleasing each other miles above the Earth—in the presence of strangers, no less—the very next morning.

Wicked, wicked Sir.

"No one is near. Stroke me harder, téa."

Brie grasped his cock and pumped it with real gusto until he gripped her wrist tightly. She heard someone pass by and whispered, "Close."

"Closer than you think," he groaned, his cock pulsing in her hand with denied release.

After the individual had returned to their seat, Sir ordered, "You're to remain still, a pleasant expression on your face, with your eyes closed. Anyone walking by will only note that there's a beautiful girl sleeping beside me."

Brie gave a slight nod.

Sir proceeded to roll his finger over her clit, wetting it with her own excitement. He teased her opening with his middle finger while he occasionally flicked his thumb over her clit. The randomness of that additional contact had her body hyper-sensitive. Each time his thumb rubbed against her, a burst of electrical energy headed straight to her core, building her sexual desire.

When he determined she was primed and ready, Sir started stroking his finger from her entrance up to the tip of her clit in slow, rhythmic motions that mimicked his long, tantalizing lick. She let out a soft gasp and he stopped.

Keeping her eyes closed, she pretended to yawn and pressed against him, hoping he would continue. After several minutes, the stroking started up again. Brie could think of nothing but the sensations his touch evoked, and the only way to assure it would continue was not to respond in any way.

Every time she heard someone pass by in the aisle, it added an extra thrill to the experience, increasing her arousal exponentially.

Normally such subtle attention would not result in an orgasm, but the exhibitionistic aspect with the added risk of being caught was an aphrodisiac for Brie. When she could take no more, her body tensed for its release.

Sir noted that she was close and started rolling his finger over her clit again, bringing her to a glorious, drawn-out orgasm. Not a peep did she make, nor did she move, as her pussy contracted and released, wetting his finger.

She felt his cock stiffen in her hand, exposing the pleasure he gained whenever he orchestrated her climax. It was intoxicating to feel the hard physical evidence of just how much he enjoyed pleasing her.

Brie opened her eyes to sneak a peek and saw Sir staring at his screen with a bored expression on his face.

No one would ever suspect the naughtiness going on under the tray tables beneath their little blanket.

Her natural inclination was to return the favor but, while still watching the screen, Sir commanded under his breath, "Remove your hand from my cock, téa."

She did so, reluctantly, because it was a direct order, but she was sad not to have the opportunity to please him more fully. Once her hand was back on her lap, Sir removed his and licked his fingers as if he'd just finished eating a delicious snack while watching his movie. He then took the water from her tray and drank it, a smile playing on his lips.

Brie quickly closed her eyes when he turned his head in her direction. She did not dare stir again until the airplane began to descend and Sir shook her shoulder.

"Wake up, my dear, the plane is about to land."

She opened her eyes to gaze into his. "Thank you, Sir," she purred.

"My pleasure, babygirl."

"You're such a sexy man…"

"And you are a very sleepy girl."

"Only for you, Sir," she answered with a grin.

"Are you ready for today?"

Brie grimaced. "I'm nervous about visiting Todd, Sir. He's such a spirited individual; I can't imagine seeing him in a hospital bed, dying."

"Brie, he cannot see your fear. You must put on a brave front, no matter what condition we find him in. He needs our strength. Anything less would be a disservice to him."

She looked down at her lap, sighing. "I hate hospitals. No… I hate the pain that happens in hospitals. They only represent death to me."

He lifted her chin. "You must be brave."

Those words reverberated through her. They were the very words Rytsar had used during their last scene together. She'd been brave then. Brie held on to that, determined to be brave now.

Faelan

Brie hesitated at the hospital entrance, frightened of what she would find inside.

"Come, Brie," Sir insisted, guiding her through the open double doors. After receiving instructions on the location of Faelan's room, they headed towards the elevators.

You must be brave... she reminded herself, straightening her posture and nodding to Sir when the elevator doors opened. He led her through several hallways until they found the room number. Outside the door stood an elderly couple, holding on to each other in a desperate embrace. Brie couldn't help wondering if they were Faelan's grandparents.

Sir walked up to the couple to introduce himself. "Mr. and Mrs. Wallace?"

They looked up, expressions of misery and hopelessness coloring their faces. The man answered matter-of-factly, "I'm Mr. Wallace."

Sir held out his hand. "It is good to finally meet you, sir. I'm Thane Davis. We've talked on the phone several times."

The woman's face lit up. "Mr. Davis?" Without warning, she threw her arms around him.

Sir embraced her, patting her lightly on the back. "Your son is going to be fine, Mrs. Wallace. He will recover from this."

It wasn't until then that Brie realized these were Faelan's parents, *not* his grandparents. The revelation was shocking, but she suspected the hardships they'd faced over the years must have taken a physical toll on the poor couple.

"Things are not well, Mr. Davis," Mr. Wallace corrected. "At this point, we're uncertain he'll even go through with the surgery."

Sir seemed surprised by the news. "What do you mean?"

Mrs. Wallace broke the hug, tears coming to her eyes. "It's like Todd's lost his will to live." A sob escaped her lips. "He refused dialysis, and now he says he doesn't want the surgery. I'm losing my boy, Mr. Davis, and there's nothing I can say or do to prevent it."

Brie swallowed the lump growing in her throat and fought off the tears, knowing that Sir was watching her. If she was going to act courageously, this was the perfect time to prove it.

"Mrs. Wallace, I'm Miss Bennett, a friend of Todd's. He has an entire community back in LA pulling for him. You're not alone."

The woman tilted her head. "You wouldn't happen to be Mary, would you?"

Brie was startled by the question, but smiled warmly.

"No, my name is Brie, but Mary and I are friends as well. Has Todd mentioned her to you?"

The woman shook her head. "No, but sometimes he calls out her name when he's asleep."

Brie had to close her eyes to keep back the tears. She opened them and smiled once she had them under control, stating with conviction, "I know we can help Todd regain his strength together. You've had far too much to handle on your own."

Mrs. Wallace broke down, sobbing as she cried on Brie's shoulder. "It's been so hard watching him…fade away."

Brie wrapped her arms around the frail woman, conveying her strength as she held her. Mr. Wallace cautioned in a low voice, "Hush, Ada. You don't want Todd hearing you through the door."

She choked back her sobs and nodded, pulling away from Brie. "I don't want to lose my son, Miss Bennett. He's been through enough in his young life. It's not fair that he's having to face this now."

"Let's concentrate on the fact that a healthy donor has been found and the operation takes place next week," Sir encouraged them. "We've come specifically to support your son. You're no longer alone in this endeavor."

"I thought Todd mentioned he had a sister," Brie said, troubled that the couple was facing this without family support.

"Lisa is in the last month of her pregnancy," Mrs. Wallace explained, new tears forming as she shared. "The doctor has restricted her to bed rest. I'm afraid the pressure of everything has gotten to her. We can't risk losing the baby too…"

"Of course not," Brie agreed, hugging her again.

"Come, Ada, let's get some coffee while Todd's friends visit," her husband suggested, taking her hand. Mr. Wallace glanced back at Sir, his face conveying a look of defeat.

Sir took Brie's hand and squeezed it. "Are you ready for this?"

He will *recover. He* will *live a long life,* she silently repeated, steeling herself for the reunion. She looked up at Sir and answered with confidence, "I'm ready, Sir."

Although Brie had thought she was ready, as the door swung open and she saw Faelan for the first time, she had to struggle to breathe.

Sir whispered, "Remember why we came."

Brie quickly pulled herself together as she took her first step into the room. Faelan looked gaunt, his face sunken and hollow. With his eyes closed, it looked as if he might already be dead—the sound of periodic gasping the only sign of life.

"Mr. Wallace," Sir said loudly. "Mr. Wallace, Miss Bennett and I have come to see you."

His eyelids fluttered for a moment, but he did not move or open them.

Brie spoke up. "Todd, it's me. Sir and I have come to visit you." When he did not respond, she called out, "Faelan."

Todd slowly opened his eyes.

Brie sucked in her breath. Those magnetic blue eyes that had always drawn her in were now dull and lifeless.

"Go away," he rasped.

Even though a chilling sense of doom fell over her, Brie stubbornly held on to her mantra. *He* will *recover. He* will *live a long life*… She shook her head, laughing softly as she took his limp hand. "Oh no, you aren't getting rid of me that easily. I'm here to stay."

He turned away slowly, a pained expression on his face. "I don't want you to see me like this. Go…now."

Brie didn't move.

"Although I appreciate how you feel, Mr. Wallace, we won't be leaving," Sir said with compassion. "You'll have to dig down deep to find the strength needed to survive this surgery, and we've come to support you in that cause."

Faelan snarled, "I don't want your help. I never asked for it."

"Friends don't wait to be asked," Brie told him.

He closed his eyes in an attempt to block her out. "I don't even want this damn operation."

"Why not?" Brie cried.

With his eyes still closed, Faelan stated coldly, "There's no point in a perfectly healthy man losing a kidney. I'm dying. Hell, I've been dying since I was sixteen. Just let me get on with it."

"You have too many people who care about you," she protested.

He laughed bitterly. "Right…"

"Don't you realize how desperate your parents are, thinking they might lose you? You can't do that to them," she insisted. "And what about your poor sister and her baby?"

He opened his eyes and glared at Brie. "They'll be better off. They *all* will."

She knew he was including Mary in that statement. Playing on his sympathy for others wasn't working, so Brie changed tactics. "What kind of legacy are you leaving if you give up now? You can't end on a cowardly note."

"I'm no coward."

"Exactly," Sir answered. "Which is why you will suffer whatever is needed to survive this. You're neither a coward nor a fool. When fate has granted you a second chance, you grab it with both hands."

When Faelan remained unmoved, Sir added in a grave tone, "You have no idea of the devastating consequences such a cowardly act would have on your family and friends."

Brie wondered if Sir was referring to his own father. Was there a part of him that resented his father for taking his life and leaving Sir behind? Her thoughts turned to Mary. Brie was concerned that if Mary ever found out Faelan had chosen to die, it might destroy her.

Without asking permission, Brie lowered the rail on the bed to sit beside Faelan. She took his hand back in hers and squeezed it. "You've touched too many lives to have the luxury of giving up now. Think who will suffer if you do—your parents, your sister, your friends…and Mary."

For the first time, she saw a flicker of light in his eyes, but he turned his head from her. "I'm tired, Brie. I just want to stop fighting." He let out a long, agonized sigh. "I just want to die in peace."

"Too fucking bad," she stated, standing back up. "I'm here now and *I* won't let you."

Faelan glanced at Sir and said in an ominous tone, "You don't want to know what I'll do to her if she stays."

"What? Are you going to throw insults at her? Because God knows you're too weak to throw anything else."

Faelan's expression darkened. "Not that long ago you wouldn't have let me near her, and *now* you're willing to risk her staying alone with me?"

"If I am brutally honest, Mr. Wallace, there's no risk involved, given your current state."

"Fuck…you."

Sir smiled. "Is that the best you can do? Brie should have no problem, then." He turned to her. "You're in charge of getting him to eat regularly and forcing him to exercise his limbs. A gratitude journal might also prove beneficial."

"You have to be shitting me," Faelan growled.

Sir replied with a straight face, "I never shit, Mr. Wallace—unless I'm in the bathroom."

Brie covered her mouth to keep from laughing.

Faelan stared at him, a look of disbelief on his face. Out of the blue, he started laughing, but it soon became gasping breaths and he turned from them in humiliation. When he finally regained his composure, he commanded hoarsely, "Go…"

"We will," Sir informed him, "but only because I need to help Brie settle in. Rest assured, Mr. Wallace, she will return tomorrow with the donor. It will give you a chance to meet the man who has graciously agreed to save your life."

Faelan stared at the window, his voice devoid of emotion. "Save us all the trouble, Mr. Davis, and buy the poor bastard a return ticket home."

His words cut Brie to the bone, but she kept her mind firmly on her mission. "So, Todd, start thinking about what you're grateful for so you can fill up your gratitude journal. Oh, and you'd better inform the nurses what you want to eat, or I will choose something for you—and I'm feeling rather spiteful at the moment."

"Go to hell, Brie."

As they exited the room, Sir smiled at her. "That went well."

"But, Sir, you saw him…"

"Mr. Wallace still has enough fight in him to give us grief. That's encouraging. I was worried for a moment."

Brie took his assertion to heart, and was able to keep a genuine smile on her face when Sir spoke to Faelan's parents. "Not to worry, Mr. and Mrs. Wallace. With Brie's caring ways, I'm certain he will not only agree to the surgery, but will recover quickly from it. You'd be surprised what's possible when you have the right people behind you."

Faelan's father shook his hand vigorously. "Thank you, Mr. Davis. Not only were you instrumental in finding our son a donor, but your support now means the world to us."

"Please save your gratitude for the donor."

"And he'll be coming tomorrow?" Mrs. Wallace asked.

"Yes. In fact, Miss Bennett will be picking him up after she drops me off at the airport. I expect he'll be here at the hospital by ten tomorrow morning."

"We'll be sure to look for him when he arrives," Mrs. Wallace assured Sir.

"Good. May I suggest you both get some rest tonight? Your son has some serious soul-searching to do, and such tasks are best done alone."

"We'll certainly take that under consideration," he replied.

Mrs. Wallace blushed as she broke away from her husband and gave Sir another hug. "Despite what you say, I can't thank you enough. You have given him—all of us, really—hope again."

"I simply made a few phone calls."

She stated shyly, "Mr. Davis, I make a strawberry jam that has won several blue ribbons at the county fair. I would like to make you some as a thank you."

He smiled down at her. "That is very kind of you. Sadly, I leave tomorrow, but if you give it to my fiancée, she'll make sure I get it."

"Very well, Mr. Davis," she agreed, returning his smile.

While they were driving to Master Anderson's home, Brie told Sir, "I love how compassionate you were with Todd's mother."

He shrugged. "I understand it's difficult to receive help without giving something back. They are such kindhearted people; it makes me curious how they will handle the gift of the donor."

"Maybe a case of strawberry jam?" Brie suggested.

Sir chuckled, ruffling her hair.

"So, Sir, did I hear that I will be picking up the man tomorrow?" Brie ventured.

"That's correct, babygirl. His flight comes in two hours after mine leaves. I must warn you, though, English is not his first language."

Brie furrowed her brow in concern, afraid of losing the hapless man in the large airport.

Sir noted Brie's expression and grinned. "No need to worry. I told him what you look like, so the pickup should go smoothly. Simply help the man with his luggage and drive him to the hospital. The staff will take it from there."

Brie nodded, satisfied with the arrangements. "Sounds simple enough."

"I've tried to make this as easy as possible for you, since I won't be here." He stared towards the impressive mountain range. "I find it extraordinary that there are people in the world willing to make that kind of sacrifice for another. Although his airfare and hospital stay are being paid for by the Wallaces, he's refused any other compensation."

Brie felt tears come to her eyes. "We're all indebted to him for this."

"Yes, we are," Sir replied, with a hint of melancholy in his voice.

Brie touched his shoulder. "Are you okay?"

"I'm sorry I won't be here, Brie."

She could tell he was genuinely distressed about it. "I'll be fine, Sir."

"I know you will," he said, gracing her with a smile.

"Did I tell you Brad has an entertaining night planned for us? Something he says will take our minds off our concerns for a while."

"Oh, my! With Master Anderson, that could mean anything." Brie giggled.

"Which is exactly why I'm looking forward to it."

Brie wondered if it would be a session in the backyard with bullwhips, or free rein over the entire Academy. Oh, the kinky possibilities!

Beta

S ir whistled as they drove up to Master Anderson's home nestled in the foothills. "He really has some view up here, doesn't he?"

"Being in the mountains overlooking the city of Denver does seem like a little slice of heaven. Boy, I can only imagine what it looks like in the winter with all that snow."

Sir snorted humorously. "The fact that I can't drive my car in the winter kills the allure of this place. He can keep his mountain paradise."

They rang the doorbell several times, and Sir banged on the door, but got no response. Brie spied Master Anderson's nosy neighbor peeking around the corner of his garage. The woman cleared her throat before stating, "Mr. Anderson is in the back, weed—" She stopped midsentence when Sir turned to face her.

"Thank you," he replied in a pleasant but formal tone.

Courtney blushed from head to toe, her attraction to Sir painfully obvious to Brie. "Are…are you a friend of

Mr. Anderson's?"

"Yes, we're long-time friends. Now if you'll excuse us." Sir put his hand on Brie's back and guided her past Courtney, heading towards the backyard.

Darned if the woman didn't blush a deep shade of red as he passed, her eyes drifting down to stare at Sir's sexy ass. Brie shook her head, stunned by the woman's brashness.

When Sir opened the backyard gate, Brie saw Master Anderson stand up in all his bare-chested glory, a handful of weeds gripped tightly in his fist. He glanced briefly at Courtney, then dropped the weeds and brushed off his hands.

The smile he bestowed on Sir as he approached was quite…beguiling.

"I don't believe it! It's really you after all this time!" He reached out to Sir, his arms outstretched.

Sir tilted his head, confused by Master Anderson's odd behavior. "I—"

"No, don't. I don't care why you left me. The only thing that matters is that you're here with me now." He wrapped Sir in his beefy arms, grabbing his ass firmly with both hands.

Sir gripped his wrists and forcefully removed the offending appendages from his butt, shaking his head with a bemused look on his face.

"Don't be like that, lover," Master Anderson scolded.

Brie heard Courtney inhale sharply behind her, and she turned to see the woman staring at the men, her mouth agape. Playing along with Master Anderson's ruse, Brie smiled nervously at Courtney as if they'd caught the lovers in a stolen moment. She slowly closed the gate on the stunned woman, blocking her from continuing to gawk.

"Come into the house," Master Anderson insisted. "I need to show you how *deeply* you've been missed." He winked at Brie as he led them into his home.

"I don't even want to ask," Sir remarked once the door was shut.

"Welcome to Ms. Courtney, the neighborhood snoop."

"Is she still trying to set you up?" Brie asked, fondly remembering the little prank they'd played on Courtney the last time she'd visited.

"I can't tell if her interest is still for others or for herself these days." He looked at Sir. "That's the reason I *had* to take advantage of your arrival."

"I hate to break it to you, Master Anderson," Brie said, laughing, "but I think you only raised the hot factor for her. I definitely saw Courtney staring with lust in her eyes when you grabbed Sir's fine ass. She might even make it her task to convert you now."

Master Anderson slapped his forehead. "I can't win with that woman."

Sir shook his head. "I don't know how you get yourself into these predicaments. I've never had any issues with my neighbors."

"Of course not. You stay in your apartment like a hermit, while I go out and actively engage my neighbors."

"More like provoke them," Sir answered, glancing at

his bare chest.

Brie giggled.

Master Anderson frowned at her. "You find this humorous, young Brie?"

"Yes, I find your situation very entertaining, Master Anderson."

He grumbled as he went to wash his hands in the sink. "Let's forget about Ms. Courtney and focus on my plans for tonight." Nodding at Brie, he said, "You'll be wearing a corset and mini-skirt for the event, and *you*…" He faced Sir. "I want you wearing dress slacks and my favorite tie, loverboy."

Sir raised an eyebrow. "What kind of place is this?"

"Ha! You're going to have to trust me, bud."

"You *are* aware I don't trust you."

Master Anderson grinned, throwing the wet hand towel at Sir. "Which is what makes this all the more fun for me."

Sir caught it nimbly and set it on the counter. "Maybe I should change my plans and take the last flight out tonight."

"Don't you dare! It's taken me *how* long to get you to come to Denver? You're not bailing out on me now."

Brie could tell Sir enjoyed having the upper hand, but also knew he liked Master Anderson far too much to follow through on his threat.

"Fine, but no more groping."

Master Anderson put his hands up the air in a gesture of surrender. "Agreed. Now why don't we head on over to the Academy? I'm anxious to show you what I've done with the place."

As they were walking out to Master Anderson's massive truck, he whispered to Brie, "Is she watching at the window?"

Brie looked back. "Affirmative."

With a sly glance at Brie, Master Anderson pinched Sir's butt.

Sir swatted his hand away in irritation. "Better watch it, Brad. I'll kiss you in front of that neighbor of yours. By the time I'm done with you, she'll be hounding you every minute of every day."

Master Anderson grinned. "I always knew you had a crush on me."

Sir laughed as he opened the passenger door for Brie. "I think it's the other way around, cowboy."

Brie giggled as she jumped into the truck, settling between the two men. How lucky was she? She didn't miss her chance to wave enthusiastically at Courtney as they drove away.

When they arrived at the Denver Academy, Sir exited the truck and stood quietly, admiring the large converted warehouse. "Okay, I am officially impressed by the size of the building."

Master Anderson took them inside, showing off the many amenities of his training center as he explained in detail everything he'd done to the place.

"Brad, this is exceptional," Sir stated when the tour was finished. "Every kind of play is possible here. What a brilliant facility."

"And the cost of the building was next to nothing," Master Anderson declared proudly.

"Your business degree certainly paid off for you."

Master Anderson nodded. "Best decision I ever made, heading back to college."

"Are you sure you can give the place up?"

Brie turned to Sir, startled by the question. Her eyes drifted over to Master Anderson as she waited for his response.

"I'd be lying if I said this was going to be easy." He caressed the back of one of the leather seats in the auditorium. "I was able to perfect what you had in LA."

"I see that."

"However, it's been difficult heading the business side of things as well as the program itself. There's a real appeal to serving only as Headmaster."

Brie stared at him, almost afraid to breathe. Was she hearing him right? Was Master Anderson coming back to the Submissive Training Center as Headmaster of the school?

"As worthy as your work here has been, there's no way to create a life outside of it. Time is your enemy, my friend."

Master Anderson raised his eyebrow. "Actually, time has been my ally."

"In avoiding life."

He chuckled. "I resemble that remark."

Sir slapped Master Anderson on the back, and they both laughed. "You've been missed, old friend, and I know the Submissive Training Center will benefit from your leadership. I said that the first time I recommended you for the position."

"Were you surprised that you weren't asked?" Master Anderson inquired as they headed back outside.

"Of course not. I stepped down from the position because I broke protocol—there's no recovering from that."

Brie looked up at him sadly, knowing she was the cause.

"Oh, no, Brie," Sir admonished. "There's no reason to feel remorse. I wouldn't give you up for a hundred Headmaster positions."

Brie said nothing, but she bound those words to her heart.

Sir turned his attention back to Master Anderson. "So what about your staff? Are any returning with you?"

It was the question Brie had been longing to ask the minute she'd heard he was returning, and she waited with bated breath to hear his answer.

"Ms. Clark is going to stay. Her previous experience at the Center makes her invaluable to this program. As for Baron, he jumped at the chance to return home."

"What about Lea?" Brie blurted.

Master Anderson smiled down at her, a look of sympathy on his face. "Ms. Taylor is still deciding."

Brie did her best to hide her disappointment. It was obvious that, as much as Lea loved her as a friend, she loved Ms. Clark more. It was a difficult truth for Brie to wrap her heart around, even though she understood it.

"Will you be returning to LA soon?" Sir inquired.

"Yes. The Training Center hasn't given me much time. Luckily, my Academy has already garnered notice in Denver, and I have a group of investors lined up to meet with me this coming week."

Sir glanced around the stylish auditorium. "Will you

be able to give this up when the time comes?"

Master Anderson gave him a smug look. "Actually, I'll be renting the facilities to the buyer at a reasonable price, while keeping the option to buy back the school at a later date."

"Smart, but you won't be returning."

"Why do you say that?"

"My gut says you aren't coming back to Denver."

Master Anderson let out a snorting laugh. "When have you ever listened to your gut?"

Sir looked down, smiling tenderly at Brie. "At least once."

"Well, I suppose if I find balance in my life, I wouldn't have a reason to come back," Master Anderson conceded.

"Precisely."

Brie trembled beside Sir while the two men talked. The mere thought of having her best friend return to LA had her all wound up, but it was the very real possibility that Lea *wouldn't* be returning that consumed her.

"Have you done any events here?" Sir asked. "This is a large enough space to take advantage of opportunities like that."

"Yes, I held a charity event not too long ago. I sponsored it with Adam Montague, co-owner of the Masters at Arms Club."

"Ah, yes, I've heard of him. A military man, correct?"

"Correct. Adam is a serious individual, but a real pleasure to work with. He even allowed his wife Karla to sing at the event—a huge hit with the donors. Sure was great seeing her on stage again…" Master Anderson shook his head, chuckling to himself. "But I have to say, babies sure change a man. I don't recommend it."

Sir cleared his throat in response to the last statement. "I assume the event was a success overall?"

"Naturally," he stated with pride. "Raised a significant amount of money for our charity. It's part of the reason I have investors chomping at the bit now."

Sir placed his hand on Master Anderson's shoulder. "I must admit, I'm looking forward to your return to LA."

"I am as well, Thane. It'll give me a chance to check on those herbs I gifted you."

Sir said nothing and looked up, appearing to examine the equipment suspended above the stage.

"Don't tell me you killed them."

Sir gave a disinterested shrug. "What did you expect? With all the traveling we've done recently, they didn't stand a chance."

"Thank goodness you aren't planning on having children," Master Anderson joked.

Brie glanced at Sir with the slightest of smiles. Although Master Anderson missed it, Sir did not, and he laughed. "Me, have children? What a ludicrous thought."

Before heading out for the evening, Sir informed Brie that he had something special to add to her outfit as he handed her a small vibrator. It was unusual, because of the silicone piece that was made to slip inside the vagina so it would fit snugly against her clit.

He explained, "Having no idea what we're doing tonight, I plan on entertaining myself." He kissed her on the lips, adding seductively, "This will *not* be a lesson in orgasm denial."

Brie quivered, knowing that meant a night of excess, and hoped she was up for the challenge. "May I put it on now?"

When he nodded, she started towards the bathroom.

"No, téa. I want to watch."

She smiled as she settled on the edge of the bed, pulling up her skirt and shimmying flirtatiously out of her panties. Brie played with herself as she glanced demurely at Sir. It was such a turn on having him watch, and soon she felt the welcome ache between her legs that made her wet enough for the toy. She picked up the vibrator and slowly slipped it inside. It rested against her pussy, much like her clit jewelry.

Sir pulled a device from his pocket and smiled at her as he switched it on. Brie jumped and then giggled as the vibration took over. She forced herself to relax as she embraced the wicked tool.

Before she could give in to the building pulsations, however, Sir turned it off, stating, "That was just a taste, babygirl. No more fun until we reach our mystery destination."

Oh, how Brie loved it when he teased her!

"Thank you for the taste, Master. I can't wait until the main course." She slipped her panties back on and stood, bowing. "I wait with impatience, but with a respectful attitude."

Sir chuckled, resting his hand on her back as he led her out of the bedroom.

Master Anderson whistled when he saw the two approach. "Now that's what I'm talking about, loverboy. The way those pants hug your tight ass is sublime, and that tie…I recall fondly what we did with that tie."

Sir fussed with the knot of his tie, grumbling, "Not sure why you insist on continuing the ruse when your neighbor isn't present to listen."

"It's all about getting into the role. Has Brie taught you nothing? She's the perfect partner when it comes to pranks. A natural at it."

Sir looked at her proudly. "Is she now?"

"Yes, and her talents are completely wasted on you."

"No," Sir replied smoothly. "I utilize those talents for a higher purpose."

"What's that?"

Sir took Brie's hand and kissed it as he stared into her eyes. "For my own pleasure."

She felt her loins contract around the toy and smiled, anxious for their night to begin.

"Enough with the lovey-dovey looks, you two," Master Anderson scolded. "It's time to roll out."

He drove them out of the foothills and into the heart of downtown Denver. The historic buildings mixed with modern chain restaurants and shopping malls were an interesting combination. He parked in a large lot that was open, but they had to walk down several streets to get to their final destination.

The old brick building was blaring music from inside,

and Brie saw a long line of people wrapped around it. She noted a small, unassuming sign hanging from the entrance, which simply read: 'Beta'.

Master Anderson walked past the line and straight up to the entrance guarded by several hunky men. One of them smiled at him in greeting. "Ah, Mr. Anderson, back so soon?"

"I have a couple of out-of-towners who have yet to enjoy the Beta experience."

"Understood. I just need to look at their IDs, but you're free to enter."

Brie looked back at the extensive line, grateful that Master Anderson had some pull. The moment the doors of the club opened, Brie was blasted with the delicious deep bass of a dubstep song. The vibration of it reverberated through her, causing her stomach to tremble with the beat.

Oh, yeah…

The thin hallway opened onto a giant concert hall. It was packed with people gyrating to the sexy beat, with laser lights and a giant disco ball above filling the room with dancing color.

Brie looked up and saw that there was a second level crowded with people looking down on them. She heard an explosion, and a flurry of confetti floated like feathers down from above.

"I love this place," she said.

"What?" Master Anderson asked, leaning closer.

She shouted, "I freaking love this place!"

Master Anderson's smile was enchanting when he replied, "I was certain you would."

He led them up a long flight of stairs to the second level. On one side of the large opening there was a line of people leaning against the railing, watching the action below, while on the other side there was a section of tables and booths, with scantily clad ladies tending their VIP clients.

Master Anderson pointed to the middle table, where a hot redhead was waiting for them. She smiled as they approached. "Mr. Anderson, what a pleasant surprise to see you again."

"You know me, Sasha. Can't resist a killer drop. The deeper the better."

She giggled sweetly. "May I ask what I can get for you and your friends?"

"I'll take my usual beer, my friend over here would like a dirty martini, and..." He looked questioningly at Brie. "What you would like?"

"I'll take a shot of Zyr vodka," she announced.

Sir nodded. "Change my order. I'll have the same."

Master Anderson looked at him in surprise. "Well, hell, if that's the case, make it three shots, Sasha."

"My pleasure."

Master Anderson sat back and smiled at them. "Have you ever been to a dance club like this?"

"No, never," Sir replied, glancing around to take it all in.

"I want to live here," Brie exclaimed, loving everything about the club—the music, the lights, as well as the erotic energy of the place.

"You have the right connections to get in most nights."

"Well, I'm glad I know you, then," she replied.

The deep, driving beat reminded Brie of Faelan and the chocolate dance they'd shared. She wondered if this was where he'd learned to love the music. Suddenly, an image of him lying in the hospital bed alone came to mind.

Sir noticed the change in her demeanor and quietly corrected her. "No, Brie. You're not allowed to think of anything but me tonight. Tomorrow will come soon enough." He reached into his pocket and she felt the buzz of the vibrator. The gentle vibration between her legs caused delicious chills to course through her body.

Brie took the shot glass Sasha handed her and looked at it critically, thinking, *A shot is a whole lot bigger in Russia.*

"Here's to a night we won't forget," Master Anderson toasted, clinking glasses with her. After she'd raised her glass to Sir and was downing the shot, her first orgasm hit. Brie squeaked, sputtering vodka.

"Straight vodka too much for you?" Master Anderson asked with amusement.

Sir smirked, turning off the vibrator. "She's perfectly fine." He kissed the remaining vodka from her lips and ordered another round.

After the second shot, Master Anderson suggested they stand by the railing to enjoy the music. Brie eagerly agreed, and was thrilled to have a chance to look down at the massive crowd below. It was one giant dance, everyone moving in rhythm to the deep bass that shook the entire building.

Brie was unaware that she was gyrating her hips in harmony with the beat until she overheard Master

Anderson tell Sir, "She's sexy when she dances."

Sir said with an appreciative smile on his lips, "This music agrees with you, téa."

"I *love* this kind of music, Sir! I can feel the energy rising up from the crowd. It's almost too much…"

He leaned down and ordered lustfully, "Dance, then, while you come for me."

Brie groaned as the vibrator caressed her clit with a new, slow, pulsating rhythm. She shuddered, not expecting the difference in vibration but responding favorably to it. Closing her eyes, she gave in to the erotic nature of the beat and swayed hypnotically to its call.

"That's it, babygirl, seduce me."

Sir's encouragement radiated through Brie. The warmth of the vodka, the tension of the vibrator and intensity of the erotic music had her floating on a sensual high, and she quickly peaked, welcoming the sensation as she orgasmed for her Master.

"Good girl," he purred in her ear. She continued to dance as the two men moved back to their seats to observe her and talk—but she noticed they did very little talking as she took on the role of exotic dancer for her Master, enticing him with her sensual moves. It was empowering, knowing she had his complete attention and the ability to drive him wild.

As she was dancing, Brie was struck by an idea she thought Sir would enjoy, so she walked over to him and whispered in his ear. He nodded his approval as he stood, moving back to the railing as he watched her leave. Brie made her way around to the other side of the large opening and threw Sir a kiss. He responded by pulsing the vibrator several times.

Brie giggled in delight, grabbing the rail to begin her seduction of him from afar. This time, laser lights of orange and yellow played across her skin, as if lighting her on fire. It was beautiful, reminding her of their fire play.

The music changed from a lively beat to one that was more slow and primal, so her movements changed accordingly. She was determined to captivate him with her alluring, cat-like grace.

Master Anderson stood beside Sir and they watched as she moved to the erotic beat. The vibrator turned back on and Brie moaned softly, giving in to Sir's desire. It was so wickedly hot to come in front of everyone, even if there was only one person watching who knew it.

Brie gripped the railing as she threw her head back and came for the third time. Afterwards she swayed her hips slowly, watching the laser lights playing across her skin and clothes as she recovered from her climax. When she looked up again, she noticed that Master Anderson had gone missing.

Sir nodded to her and gestured, but she was unsure of his meaning. Taking it as a command to keep dancing, Brie started up again, her focus solely on him. She felt someone brush up beside her and turned to see a young man wearing a black T-shirt and a lustful stare. She scooted to the left but he followed her, pressing even closer.

All of a sudden, she was encased by two strong arms grasping the railing on either side of her, effectively trapping her. She would have been concerned, but she knew those arms well.

"Scram," Master Anderson told the boy. "This one's mine."

The young man looked up at his impressive stature and shrugged, disappearing into the moving mass of people without a word.

"We saw him descending on you," Master Anderson informed Brie.

"I was oblivious."

"We could tell."

Brie giggled and looked back to ask him, "Should I head back?"

"No, your Master wants you to dance a little longer."

She looked over the expanse and saw Sir nod. Brie started up again, but with less hip action, conscious of Master Anderson being so close.

The vibrator buzzed back to life, and she moaned in surprise.

Master Anderson bent down. "What was that?"

She shook her head as the buzzing increased. Sir gestured that she should continue dancing. As she began to sway, Master Anderson moved with her, the two becoming one unit as they responded to the deep, pulsing bass.

It was erotic to be in the protective embrace of Master Anderson as she danced for Sir. Every now and then their bodies touched briefly and the slight contact sent shivers through her.

When the vibrations increased in power, Brie knew Sir was demanding an orgasm from her. Although Master Anderson was close, Brie licked her lips and let the delicious feeling take hold. She lost herself in it, letting her carnal desire take over her reservations, the music almost demanding it.

Brie whimpered when she started to come, then felt Master Anderson crush her against the railing, growling, "As per your Master's orders."

The rigidness of his erect cock pressing against her ass caused Brie to climax powerfully. He wrapped her in his arms until her trembling stopped, before pulling away and offering his hand to her.

"Shall we return to your Master?"

Brie was a little unsure on her feet, so Master Anderson held her tight, providing the extra support needed to walk.

"Lovely," Sir complimented as Master Anderson handed her over. "I enjoyed watching that little scene play out."

"Fortunately, I got there in time," Master Anderson stated.

Sir smiled at Brie. "She can get a little distracted when she's determined to please me."

Master Anderson shifted his tight jeans, his impressive erection visibly straining against his pants. "Why don't I order you another round while I search out a girl to…dance with," he said with a cheeky grin.

"By all means, my friend," Sir agreed.

When Sasha brought them another round of vodka, Sir raised his glass to Brie. "Here's to our small attempt to get Brad back in the game."

Brie clinked her glass against his in admiration. "You are a clever one, Sir."

They didn't return to the house until the wee hours

of the morning. Master Anderson seemed unusually quiet and content on the drive home—a good sign, Brie thought.

When she finally made it to the bedroom, Brie felt an overwhelming need to jump on Sir. "Let me please you as much as you pleased me, Master."

"Oh, you will," he assured her. "I've just been priming you for the event. Two days of making you come while denying myself has made me a ravenous man."

She stood and watched as he undressed, starting with his tie. He was slow and deliberate in his movements. Brie literally shivered as she watched him slide it off, then unbutton his shirt.

"What's wrong, babygirl?"

"I want to please you so badly, Sir."

He smiled. "Orgasming multiple times wasn't enough for you?"

"Not when you couldn't join in the fun."

"Come, then, and show me the level of your desperation."

Having his permission, Brie held nothing back as she pushed him against the wall, struggling to undo his pants. Sir lifted her chin and kissed her forcefully as she tugged on his boxers, releasing his cock from its confinement.

She fell to her knees and grasped his shaft in her hand, gratefully wrapping her lips around it as she began to bob up and down on his cock.

Sir was a bundle of tense muscles and she could feel him shuddering as she released her passion on his manhood.

"Brie…"

She looked up at him, his shaft still in her mouth. "Slower."

She smiled as she released his cock and nibbled and licked up the side of it and back down. She took his balls in her mouth one at a time and sucked lightly, before grazing the length of his shaft with her teeth.

His growl of lust made her pussy even wetter. She opened her mouth and took the fullness of him down her throat, but he pulled her back. "No, we're not going there tonight. On the bed, all fours."

He pulled her up and pushed her towards the bed. She presented herself to him, knowing her pussy was wet and swollen with need. She didn't look back, waiting for him to take her, wondering if Sir had forgotten his vow in his desire for satisfaction.

He grasped her ass with his powerful hands, bruising her flesh as he ripped the vibrator from her. But he suddenly stopped, growling to himself. "Fuck!"

She heard Sir frantically rummaging through his suitcase. "Where is it, damn it?" When she moved to get up to help, he commanded, "Stay there—don't you dare move."

Brie returned to her position, arching her back just a little more to entice him. He murmured his approval. "Very nice. Play with yourself while you wait for me."

Soon she heard the slippery sound of lubricant and smiled to herself. He was not breaking his vow, but she was grateful he would be fucking her deeply. He played with her ass using his thumbs, spreading her cheeks apart to admire the pink rosette that would soon take the length of him.

Sir sucked in his breath as he pressed the head of his

cock against the tight muscles of her sphincter. Her burning desire for him was sated as he slowly slipped inside. "I love watching your ass take my shaft."

Brie closed her eyes as he pulled out only to push in again. "Master, I love the feeling of possession it evokes."

He thrust deeper. "Then feel the fullness of my possession."

When Brie cried out, Sir covered her mouth and warned, "We're not at home, babygirl."

He kept his hand on her mouth as he ramped up his thrusting. Brie's muffled moans filled the bedroom as Sir made demands on her body. He fucked her hard, being completely selfish in his taking of her, and Brie savored it.

When he let out a low, guttural cry, Brie felt Sir stiffen as he filled her ass with his seed. He collapsed on top of her afterwards, panting, "I needed that more than you know."

She turned her head and smiled. "I did too, Sir, more than you know."

He kissed her on the lips and lifted himself off, lying down beside her. "This separation may be harder than I anticipated." He tenderly caressed her face. "Damn, I will miss you."

A tear rolled down her cheek as she nodded in agreement.

"Only two more months," he reminded her.

"Two months."

"And then I'll make my fucking count."

Brie burst into giggles and hugged him.

The Donor

B rie sighed heavily the next day when the moment came to say goodbye at the security line.

"Keep in mind your purpose, Brie. You're exactly what Mr. Wallace needs right now. Trust your instincts. Others have caved under the weight of his situation, but you know him better than most and you understand what he has to live for."

"I won't forget that, Sir, no matter how difficult it gets."

"As for me, I hope for a quick resolution with Lilly concerning my mother, but that is probably wishful thinking on my part. It'll be a shock when she sees the Beast, and there's that whole process of letting go…"

"How long do you think you'll be there?"

"I'm hoping not more than a week. However, if Lilly decides to end her life, I'm afraid we'll be there much longer while she comes to terms with that choice."

"I don't know which I should hope for, Sir."

"I would prefer to end her life, no matter how long it takes. This holding on when she's already gone has been torture for me. I don't wish that on Lilly." Sir looked at his watch. "I need to go."

"I know," Brie choked out, trying unsuccessfully to hold back the tears.

Sir wiped them away. "No crying, babygirl. Be strong. At night, when you are alone and your thoughts are with me, *then* you can cry freely into your pillow. Connect with me whenever you feel sad and I will be your comfort."

She nodded, lowering her head so he wouldn't see her tears. Sir lifted her chin and kissed the remaining ones away. "Enough," he whispered. His gentle attention and feather-light kisses made her smile, despite her sorrow. "That's better, babygirl."

More for herself than for him, she declared, "I will not fail, Sir."

"I have no doubt you will succeed and you have others here you can lean on, but remember I am your man—the rock you can count on. I don't want anyone else playing that role for you."

"Yes, Sir."

"While waiting to pick up the donor, I want you to eat something. I noticed you didn't touch your food this morning."

She laughed sadly. "I never feel hungry the day you leave."

"Nevertheless, you will eat now, and I expect you to continue to eat three meals a day while I'm gone—whether you're hungry or not. Agreed?"

She nodded, loving him all the more for caring so much.

Brie watched Sir go, comforting herself with the thought that she could cry later that night. She waited until he'd disappeared down the escalator to the underground transport train before she made her way to the food court. Even though the thought of eating made her nauseous, she dutifully bought a salad and ate it with the plastic fork provided. She stared at the instrument afterwards, imagining Sir raking it down her back like a Wartenberg wheel. It made her smile, so she stuffed the utensil in her purse.

She felt a sense of renewed confidence, certain she would prove worthy of Sir's faith in her. The sobering fact was Faelan could not afford her to fail.

When the time came, Brie headed toward the exit area for the arriving passengers and waited nervously for the donor. Sir hadn't told her what he looked like, so she was counting on the fact that he would recognize her. Every time a new group of people emerged from the underground station, she searched their faces, hoping to see a spark of recognition.

Two young children, who were waiting for their father's plane to arrive, started running in circles around Brie out of sheer boredom. The little boy accidentally bumped into her, causing Brie to stumble where she stood. He looked up at her in alarm and then ran behind his mother for protection.

"Tell the nice lady you're sorry for running into her," his mother demanded.

The little boy shook his head.

Pulling him from behind her, the mother said in a harsher tone, "Do it, *now*."

Brie felt sorry for the boy and knelt down, saying, "It's okay. I was getting bored too."

The boy smiled, his ears turning a shade of pink, before he darted behind his mother again.

Brie stood up and assured the woman that further apology was unnecessary, but stopped mid-sentence when she heard her name called behind her.

"Brie…"

Her heart skipped a beat as she turned and looked into those warm, chocolate-brown eyes she knew so well. She shook her head, not quite believing he was standing there before her.

Tono Nosaka walked around the barrier and took her hand, shaking it formally. "It is a pleasure to meet you, Miss Bennett."

"Are you Todd's donor?"

He smiled with a glint in his eye. "It seems fate has brought us together again."

She couldn't stop smiling as she led him to the baggage claim area. There was so much to ask, so much she needed to know, but she couldn't satisfy her curiosity in such a public arena, so she was forced to wait.

To bide her time, she kept glancing at him, blushing whenever he caught her staring. The Asian Dom was still just as handsome as she remembered, with his long, dark bangs and gentle smile.

She couldn't believe Tono was here. *Sneaky Sir,* she giggled to herself, knowing he had purposely orchestrated this surprise for her.

Once the luggage had been loaded into the rental car and they'd both buckled up, Brie turned to Tono and begged, "Please tell me everything!"

He chuckled. "Everything? Why don't I condense it down for you?"

"As long as you don't leave out any important parts, like what happened to your mother, and how did Chikako take the news of you leaving, and are you here to stay? Please say you are!"

He shook his head, his eyes sparkling with amusement. "I will tackle them one question at a time, but I suggest you start the car or we'll never leave this place."

Brie turned the key and revved up the engine, heading out of the parking garage before declaring, "Okay, you can begin."

"You're aware my mother remains a forceful personality, and I'm unable to bear it like my father did. Things had gotten so bad between us that I spent most of my time away from the family home simply to avoid the constant bickering."

Brie looked at him with compassion. "I'm so sorry, Tono."

"Slow down, Brie," he said in a quiet, unruffled voice.

She turned to look at the road and had to slam on her brakes to avoid hitting the car in front of her that had switched lanes unexpectedly. With her heart racing, she let off the brake and hit the gas again.

"Please continue."

"Keep your eyes on the road."

"Yes, yes. I will," she promised.

With her verbal assurance given, Tono continued. "When Sir Davis called to inform me of Wallace's condition, I was at a loss. I knew our blood types matched, which is exceedingly rare, but I was unsure if I was in a position to help. When I broached the subject with my mother, something very odd but fortuitous happened. She refused to talk to me for a week. I naturally assumed she was angry and would forbid me from shirking my duty to her." Tono smiled, shaking his head. "But I couldn't have been more wrong."

His words were like music to her ears. "Oh, my goodness, what did she do?"

"Brie, look ahead," he cautioned.

She glanced back in time to see a family of ducks crossing the road. She instinctively swerved to miss them and nearly hit the car beside her.

"That's it!" she cried in frustration.

Brie took the next exit and parked on the shoulder, positioning the car so they were facing west, towards the outline of blue-and-white peaks in the distance. "I can't wait to hear this until we get to the hospital to hear this, and I'll kill us if I continue driving."

He chuckled softly, nodding his agreement. "Always impetuous, but only because of your true heart."

Brie grasped his arm, begging, "Please, Tono, tell me what happened with your mother."

He smiled, but the emotion did not transfer to his eyes. "When she finally spoke to me, I was told I had never been a good son."

Brie sputtered in disbelief. "But...but..."

"It wasn't said in anger, it was simply her truth. I was never what she wanted or needed. She and I are like oil and water."

"But you've done *everything* she's asked. You sacrificed your life for her!"

"It was a healthy revelation, Brie. I did not mind hearing it."

"You have to know what she said is untrue, Tono. You are an incredible son, and a remarkable person."

He caressed her cheek, releasing the tension from her face. "The beauty of that admission is that it set me free. There was no more point in trying to please her."

"But she's wrong," Brie insisted.

"No, Brie. It is her reality, as well as mine. She's never been the mother I needed. When she insisted I leave Japan, it was the first time I didn't resent submitting to her will."

Brie growled in justified anger. "But she should have thanked you for everything you've done, all the sacrifices you made."

"Letting me leave was enough. Who knew that the Boy would end up being my ticket to freedom?" Tono's genuine smile lightened her heart. "Life is a beautiful mystery."

Brie looked deeply into his eyes, noting the joy as well as the sorrow she found there. "How did Chikako take the news of your leaving?"

"That was not easy," he said. Tono looked towards the mountains as he confessed, "We'd grown close, working together. There is an intimate bond created with the jute."

"I know," Brie said with quiet conviction.

He had a look of remorse when he said, "I think for the first time I understand the dynamic you share with the Boy. I care for Chikako, and I thoroughly enjoy her company, but…"

"What?"

"I will never love her."

"Your parting could not have been easy for either of you."

The pain in his voice tugged at her heart. "No, it wasn't. For the first time, I know what it is to break a heart."

"Still, you were kind."

Tono frowned, shaking his head. "There is no kind way to break a person's heart."

She reached out, touching his shoulder in sympathy. "Does that mean you left on bad terms?"

"Chikako saw me off at the airport and assured me she was okay…but I know better."

Brie gazed deep into his eyes. There was so much left unsaid, things that could never be spoken between them.

"As to your last question, I will be staying. I'm unsure where I will settle down after the surgery, but Japan is not in my future."

"I'm glad, Tono."

He stared at her, those gentle eyes expressing a torrent of emotion. Finally, he spoke. "So now we must go and see if the Boy will accept my offer."

"Wait! Todd doesn't know you're the donor?"

"Sir Davis and I agreed it was best, considering the past history I shared with the Boy. The simple fact is that Wallace has no more options. We've placed him against the wall, knowing he will resist." Tono smiled at her tenderly. "Which is where you come in."

"I don't have that kind of power over Todd. Not anymore."

"You have more than you think. Used in the right way, it may prove lifesaving."

"But if I fail…"

"There's no fear of that. You and I will convince the Boy that his life is more important than his willful self-pity."

Brie started up the car again, but said one more thing before she started off. "I'm worried for you, Tono. This isn't an easy operation and there are risks." She turned to face him. "Even if it goes well, you won't be able to perform your art for months after recovery. And worse, what if years down the road your remaining kidney fails?"

"I understand what lies ahead for me, and I accept the risks."

Tears came to Brie's eyes, but she held them at bay. "Your mother is blind, Tono. You are an exceptional human being." She backed up and threw the car into drive, speeding towards the hospital—and what would become Tono's destiny.

What has fate planned for the gentle Kinbaku Master?
Enjoy the romance and emotional ride of *Claim Me*.

Buy the next in the series:

#1 (Teach Me)

#2 (Love Me)

#3 (Catch Me)

#4 (Try Me)

#5 (Protect Me)

#6 (Hold Me)

#7 (Surprise Me)

#8 (Trust Me)

#9 (Claim Me)

#10 (Enchant Me)

Brie's Submission series:

You can find Red on:
Twitter: @redphoenix69
Website: RedPhoenix69.com
Facebook: RedPhoenix69

 Keep up to date with the newest release of Brie by signing up for Red Phoenix's newsletter: redphoenix69.com/newsletter-signup

Red Phoenix is the author of:

Blissfully Undone

* Available in eBook and paperback

(Snowy Fun—Two people find themselves snowbound in a cabin where hidden love can flourish, taking one couple on a sensual journey into ménage à trois)

His Scottish Pet: Dom of the Ages

* Available in eBook and paperback

Audio Book: *His Scottish Pet: Dom of the Ages*

(Scottish Dom—A sexy Dom escapes to Scotland in the late 1400s. He encounters a waif who has the potential to free him from his tragic curse)

The Erotic Love Story of Amy and Troy

* Available in eBook and paperback

(Sexual Adventures—True love reigns, but fate continually throws Troy and Amy into the arms of others)

eBooks

Varick: The Reckoning

(Savory Vampire—A dark, sexy vampire story. The hero navigates the dangerous world he has been thrust into with lusty passion and a pure heart)

Keeper of the Wolf Clan (Keeper of Wolves, #1)

(Sexual Secrets—A virginal werewolf must act as the clan's mysterious Keeper)

The Keeper Finds Her Mate (Keeper of Wolves, #2)

(Second Chances—A young she-wolf must choose between old ties or new beginnings)

The Keeper Unites the Alphas (Keeper of Wolves, #3)

(Serious Consequences—The young she-wolf is captured by the rival clan)

Boxed Set: Keeper of Wolves Series (Books 1-3)

(Surprising Secrets—A secret so shocking it will rock Layla's world. The young she-wolf is put in a position of being able to save her werewolf clan or becoming the reason for its destruction)

Socrates Inspires Cherry to Blossom

(Satisfying Surrender—a mature and curvaceous woman becomes fascinated by an online Dom who has much to teach her)

By the Light of the Scottish Moon

(Saving Love—Two lost souls, the Moon, a werewolf and a death wish…)

In 9 Days

(Sweet Romance—A young girl falls in love with the new student, nicknamed 'the Freak')

---

9 Days and Counting

(Sacrificial Love—The sequel to In 9 Days delves into the emotional reunion of two longtime lovers)

And Then He Saved Me

(Saving Tenderness—When a young girl tries to kill herself, a man of great character intervenes with a love that heals)

Play With Me at Noon

(Seeking Fulfillment—A desperate wife lives out her fantasies by taking five different men in five days)

Connect with Red on Substance B

Substance B is a platform for independent authors to directly connect with their readers. Please visit Red's Substance B page where you can:

- Sign up for Red's newsletter
- Send a message to Red
- See all platforms where Red's books are sold

Visit Substance B today to learn more about your favorite independent authors.

CPSIA information can be obtained
at www.ICGtesting.com
Printed in the USA
LVOW04s1958211016
509751LV00008B/425/P

9 780692 772584